Young Money
Volume 1 Rags To Riches

By Darius Christian

D. Christian

Thank you for taking time out to read my book, "Young Money". I hope you enjoy the book. Also, please do a book review on Amazon.com to let me know what you think.

Young Money

Bottom Life Publishing 1624
bottomlifepublishing1624@yahoo.com

Cover Design By:
Chanel Smith
WPD Media

D. Christian

Printed in the United States of America

Dedication

This book is dedicated to my mother Sandra Christian Cotton. She is the reason I have never felt alone or like there was something that I could not do. And to my Lord and Savior Jesus Christ, who gave me the faith to know that everything is possible through God. I would also like to thank my sister Tenesha Gray and her husband Greg, my Aunt Joann, Aunt Peggy, and my stepfather Mike Cotton, the only man I've ever called Dad. Also, my brothers Wayne, Terence, Shawn, Herb, and my niece and nephews Ja'Niel, Jadyn, Gregory, and Donovan. Thank you to my two mini me's, my daughter Shamari and my son Keenan, who have helped me feel so far more important than the man that I am, because of the love that we share with one another. I love you two so very much and thank you both for allowing me to be in your lives.

Chapter 1

It's Tuesday morning, schools out for teacher's conferences, and it's already 80 degrees and humid when Devin is awakened by his mom.

"Devin, I am leaving for work now and this house better be clean when I get home, and make sure my doors are locked when you leave to go to the Boys Club."

"Ok Mom. Love you!" Devin stretches his arms above his head and yawns, as he jumps out of bed to look out the window at his mom leaving for work.

The sun is blinding and the housing projects across the street are already alive with kids playing, dope fiends fiendishly looking for their next hit of dope, and the hustlers running their everyday operations. Looking out his bedroom window was like watching a movie. Devin was so fascinated by the hustlers in the projects doing their thing, that he didn't notice his best friend Vincent crossing the street.

"Yo D! Yo! Damn homie, you deaf or something? Snap out! Your mom is gone already right? Open the door!" Vincent barked up at Devin, who was still staring out the open window.

Vincent and Devin have been best friends since the first grade. Vincent lived in the projects across the street and hated to come over to Devin's house when his mom was home. Vincent thought that she was mean, because she never allowed Devin to come into the housing projects to his house. When Devin would ask to come over, she would always say no with no explanation no nothing, just straight up no, and Vincent never understood why.

BAM! BOOM! BOOM! Devin was so anxious to get down the stairs to let Vincent in, that he didn't notice he had left his play station in the middle of the room. He fell to the floor hard with the controller cords twisted around his ankles.

"Ouch!" Devin rubbed his head that he bumped on the corner of his bed post. "Damn that hurt," he said to himself, as he finished untangling the cords from around his ankles and headed downstairs to open the door. "What up V?"

"I'm good. Just holding it down. What's up with you daydreaming in the window and shit?"

"Why you up all early asking all these questions and shit?" Asked Devin, closing the door behind his friend.

"Man, the po-pos woke me up this morning, knocking at the door all hard and shit; scared the shit out of me. I thought I was dreaming at first, until I got out of bed and looked out the window at two white faces looking at me peeking through the curtains. So, I had to open the door and see what they wanted. That's when they started talking some shit nonstop about they found a dead body by the trash dumpster, and they wanted to know if I or anybody else heard or seen something."

"What did you tell 'em?"

"What do you mean what did I tell 'em! Snitches get stitches. I said I didn't see or hear nothing and that my mom was at work."

"When did your mom get a job?" Devin asked, with a puzzled look on his face.

"D don't play, you know my mom ain't got no damn job. I couldn't tell them that. I haven't seen my mom in two days though."

"True that! So, what's good for today?" Asked Devin.

"Get dressed! We need to get some money; collect some bottles or something before we go to the club."

Empty bottles returned to Chubb's Grocery Store were twenty-five cents a bottle. This was Vincent and Devin's hustle to get money, so they could play arcade games at the Boys Club.

Lunch and dinner at the Boys Club was free, and most parent's in the neighborhood were thankful for that. There were plenty of days Devin and Vincent would have to eat at the club or go hungry. Either because Devin's mom had to work overtime at her second job or Vincent's mom was M.I.A, on one of her crack binges.

After Devin washed his face and brushed his teeth, he put on a pair of Dickie shorts, a white T, and his white Chuck Taylors. Even though Devin didn't have much gear to choose from, he coordinated what he did have so well, that he always looked good in his clothes.

Two hours later Vincent and Devin enter Chubb's Grocery Store with six-dollars' worth of bottles to trade in that they had collected around the neighborhood; some found, and some stolen off of back porches.

"I hope Sharonda's mom is working. Ms. Hall is thick!" Said Vincent.

"I know that's right. She looks good for an old woman and her body is like BOW!" Devin gestured, with his hands.

"Sharonda is a thicky thick too!"

"She gets it from her momma." Devin said, as they started laughing and giving each other a pound. They were both all smiles, as they placed their bottles onto the counter and noticed Ms. Hall, who had her back to them, giving them a perfect view of her perfectly round apple bottom frame. Ms. Hall's body was banging like always, small waist and thick thighs to go with her long legs. To be her age she had the perfect figure. Devin and Vincent were both standing at the counter in a trance; eyes all over Ms. Hall's perfect frame when she suddenly turned around and caught them staring.

"What are you two doing?" Asked Ms. Hall.

"Nothing! I mean trying to cash these bottles in," Vincent said, embarrassed.

"Are you Mrs. Cotton's son?"

"Yes, that's my mom," answered Devin.

"Tell your mom I said hello!" Ms. Hall said, as she counted out six dollars and handed it to Devin.

Devin and Vincent split the money and then took one more look at Ms. Hall. "Damn!"

"Yo! V where you going?" Devin turned to catch up with Vincent.

"I need to go down aisle three real quick. Keep a look out for me," Vincent said, grabbing a box of Arm & Hammer baking soda off the shelf and tucking it into his pants.

"Why you stealing baking soda fool?" Devin asked, confused.

"It's for the Cali boys that stay a couple doors down from me. For some reason they always send me to the store for this stuff, plus they pay me to go."

"Say no more. I am definitely down with making money." Devin said, before stealing a box also.

"Come on let's grab some chips and sodas and get up out of here."

Devin was a little nervous standing in the checkout line, and felt so relieved when they were out of the store. He wasn't scared of nothing, but

Vincent knew the last time Devin got caught stealing, his mom almost beat the black off his ass.

"One of these days we not gonna have to steal. We're gonna have enough money to get whateva we want." Devin said, as they walked down 16th Street headed to Vincent's.

When they got to 16th and Lake Street, they ran into one of the older boys from the housing projects named Tray. A lot of people were afraid of him because of his short temper and violent ways. Tray had this glass eye that would freak Devin out, because sometimes he would pull it out. Everybody knew not to make fun of his glass eye though.

Devin could remember the time that he watched Tray beat a man almost to death because he thought that the guy was staring and making fun of his eye. Actually, the guy did call him a pirate jokingly, but when he kept on and called him, Slick Rick, the joke was over, and Tray beat the shit out of him. So, it was hard for Devin to look him in the face when they talked.

"Yo! What's up Lil Homies?" Tray asked, from the doorway at the abandoned building. He seemed to be hiding in the cuts.

"What's up O. G.?" Asked Vincent.

"What up?" Devin said, giving Tray a pound without looking him in the face.

"Why y'all not in school Little Homies?"

Before they could answer him, a police cruiser turned onto the block, and Tray vanished like magic.

"Damn! What's up with Tray?" Asked Devin.

"Probably got a warrant or something?" Vincent said, as they continued walking down 16th Street.

"V, you want to stop on Victor Street and see what's up with Jazz?" Jazz was one of their partners from school who lived on Victor Street. Jazz was spoiled. He had all the Jordan's and latest gear. He lived with his grandparents, uncle, and two sisters.

"Yeah, that's cool!" Vincent said, downing the last of his grape soda.

When Devin and Vincent reached Victor block, Jazz was already outside shooting some baskets. Jazz had a basketball hoop on the garage to their house, which wasn't normal for the area.

"What up Jazz?" Vincent and Devin asked, as they walked up the driveway

"What y'all doing on the block?" Jazz asked, then passed the ball to Devin, who spotted up and shot a jump shot that went in all net.

"Sswisssh! My new jumper, pure like orange juice fool." Devin said, laughing while giving Jazz a fist pound.

All three boys knew each other had nice basketball games. Shit, everybody in the neighborhood thought the three boys were the most promising to make it to college and then the NBA. They were that good. They had been playing basketball together or against each other for years, either at the Boys Club or Kellom Elementary School across from the projects.

Jazz and Devin played for the Boys Club, and Vincent and Chuck played for Kellom. During the summer AAU tournament, they all would play for the same team (Pearl) for coach Kenny.

"What brings you my way?" Jazz asked.

"Just came from Chubbs, about to go to the club and ball when we come from V's," said Devin.

"Hold up while I go ask my grandma if I can go."

"Hurry up fool," said Vincent.

Jazz came out the house still carrying his basketball. "Let's go!"

"Leave that basketball. We are gonna stop by Vincent's before we go to the club."

"I'm working on my dribble game," Jazz said, ignoring Devin's request, while dribbling the basketball as they walked down the street, headed to the projects.

Chapter 2

Nicknamed Little Vietnam, The Logan Fontenelle Housing Projects are known to be the worst and most notorious projects in Nebraska. The Omaha Police Department hesitated to come to calls when dispatched to them because of their officers being killed there, more than once.

This was Jazz's first time going inside the projects. He had passed by plenty of times in a car and had seen them plenty of times on the news, but this was his first time stepping on the grounds of Little Vietnam. Right from the start before they passed the first unit, Jazz felt uneasy, and the screaming, yelling, cursing, and things breaking, coming from 2312 didn't calm his jitters any. No one else paid any attention to it or the calls for help. It's sad to say, but domestic abuse in the projects was the norm, along with gun shots and drug deals.

2312 was known for the screaming, yelling, and cursing. Mr. Howard had a habit of beating on his wife. Things had only gotten worse since their son was killed. Mr. Howard had started drinking heavier and the fighting was much more frequent, without anyone to stop the abuse. You would think a woman would leave after so much abuse, but like they say, "love is a crazy thing." In the projects it was a rule of some sort not to get involved in anyone else's business, and do not call or talk to the police. So basically, Mrs. Howard was on her own.

"Damn! Y'all hear that?" Asked Jazz, confused as to why nobody else was paying any attention. "Sounds like somebody's getting they ass beat."

"That's just Mr. and Mrs. Howard. They are always fighting." Vincent said, as they continued to walk towards his house on the other side of the ballfield.

The Vietnam Projects were also the largest housing projects in Nebraska. The 500 units and over 2000 residents from 20ᵗʰ Street to 24ᵗʰ Street seemed to stretch for miles. There was a football field, swing sets, a sand pit, baseball diamond, and basketball courts right in the middle of the projects. Next to the basketball courts was one of the most popular and most dangerous drug areas in Nebraska called, "Crack Alley" where there was traffic twenty-four hours a day.

Any and everything could be purchased in Crack Alley from sex, to guns, pills, promethazine with coding, heroin, dope, and especially crack cocaine. Anything you wanted illegal was in Crack Alley all the time. The Logan Fontenelle Projects were a city within a city.

"Hey Little Homies, let me see that ball!" A couple of older kids called out from the bleachers of the baseball diamond, just before Vincent, Jazz, and Devin crossed the ballfield to the other side of the housing projects.

Trying their best to ignore the call for Jazz's basketball, the boys just kept walking; that is until the rough looking dude from the bleachers ran up on them. He looked to be about eighteen or nineteen years old.

"Y'all can't hear or something? I said let me see that ball, before I take it."

"You ain't taking nothing from us fool!" Devin said sternly, figuring together they could whoop the kid; until the kid pulled a rusty looking gun from underneath his shirt.

"Yo Muff, what cha doing fool? Leave those kids alone blood." The other guy in the bleachers yelled.

"I was just fuckin wit 'em, we can't have no punks running around in these projects."

"That's my bad, my homeboy is burnt out. What's y'alls names? I see y'all around the hood all the time. I like how y'all ride for each other. My name is Pookie and this brazy fool is Muff," said the other guy from the bleachers, when he came over holding a 24oz bottle of Corona.

"I...I...I'm Jazz!" Jazz said, eyes wide still looking at the gun in the kid's hand.

"I'm Devin!" Devin said, flaming mad because he told Jazz not to bring the basketball.

"I know you. You Killa Mike's son?"

"Yeah!" Vincent said, proud to be known as his dad's son.

"Your dad was a good dude. He made sure everybody in these projects' families were straight. He was a real money getter. If y'all eva need something, holla at me," Pookie said, before he walked back to the bleachers.

"I told you not to bring that ball. Damn!" Devin exhaled.

"Let's go! There go Cali and dem right there," Vincent pointed at three sporty dressed dudes, wearing mostly red everything from their Jordan's to their starter caps. They even had red dickie shorts that Devin had never seen before. "Hey Cali, what's up?"

"What's up Lil V. My name is Taco, Lil Homie, not Cali."

"My bad Big Homie. I got something fo' you." Vincent was about to pull the baking soda out of his pants until Taco stopped him.

"Come on inside. I need you to go to McDonalds for us. So, what's your homies' names? I see y'all rollin deep." Taco said, closing the door behind Jazz, who was the last one to come inside.

"That's Jazz, and that's Devin with the baking soda." Vincent pointed at Jazz and Devin holding the box of baking soda.

"Thanks for the soda, but I don't need all that." Taco laughed to himself, looking at the Arm and Hammer box in Devin's hand.

"That's cool. I was only trying to make a little money too," said Devin.

"I'm still gonna keep it, but why make a little money when you can make a lot?" Taco asked, grabbing the box of soda from Devin, then pulling the biggest wad of money Devin, Vincent, and Jazz had ever seen out his pocket. "I need y'all to go to McDonalds for us. Is that bool?"

"Yeah, we gotcha Big Homie."

"Hey Black and J.R.! Y'all want something from McDonalds?" Taco turned and asked his two friends.

"Yeah, get me two double cheeseburgers, a large fry, and something to drink," J.R. said, giving Devin a twenty-dollar bill.

"Get me a twelve-piece McNugget, a large fry, and a couple apple pies," Black said, giving Jazz twenty dollars from his large roll of money.

"Vincent, you already know what I want. Do I need to write it down for y'all?"

"Nah, I got it."

"Oh yeah stop at the corner store, and grab a couple boxes of sandwich bags," Taco said, opening the front door to let them out.

Devin, Vincent, and Jazz were excited about the money they would make for their little walk to McDonalds.

"Did you see all that money? We all are gonna make about twelve dollars off this trip."

"Forget twelve dollars. I want my own bankroll like theirs." Devin said to Vincent.

All the way to McDonalds and back the boys talked about what they would do if they had big bank rolls of money. They were still talking and laughing about their daydreams of what they would do if they were rich, when they returned from McDonalds.

When the boys shut the door behind them and walked into the living room, they noticed Black playing NBA Live on the biggest TV they had ever seen. The picture was so large and clear that the boys just stared with their eyes glued to it.

Taco was in the kitchen over the stove cooking something and J.R. was at the kitchen table chopping up something hard and white with a razor.

"Yo! Did you get the sandwich bags?" Devin sat the bags of food on the table, then tossed J.R. the sandwich bags.

"Look up under that couch and give me that scale." J.R. said, still concentrating on what he was doing at the table.

"This?" Vincent asked, as he pulled the digital scale from underneath the couch.

"Yeah, that's it!" Black said, never taking his eyes off the game he was playing.

"Black, bring your lazy ass over here and help me bag this shit up," barked J.R.

D. Christian

"Damn! Here I come. Y'all want to play Little Homies?" Black asked, tossing the controller to Jazz before he grabbed the scale from Vincent, and headed over to the table to help J.R.

Devin had more interest in what was going on at the table and in the kitchen than he did the game.

"Pssst. Taco what's up with youngsta? Why he watching us so hard?" Black whispered.

"It's cool, he's probably soaking up the game. They are always around here doing this or that, hustling everybody for a dollar or two."

"I see you looking little man. What's up?" Black gestured for Devin to come over to the table.

Devin didn't want to appear to be lame to what they were doing by asking questions. He had heard of drugs and all the money you could make selling them, but he had never seen any drugs, besides the weed that his mom smoked sometimes. "What's up?" Devin asked, eyes glued to everything that was going on at the table in the kitchen.

"Don't fuck with this shit right here Youngsta. It will fuck your life up; I don't care if you're selling it or using it. Don't get me wrong, you can get rich selling it though." Black said, seriously.

"And be ready for the problems that come with it," added J.R.

"So, what's that for?" Devin pointed to the scale.

"To weigh the dope. You see these right here? These are quarters; seven grams on the scale. One-gram sales for a hundred dollars. Those right there are half ounces; fourteen grams on the scale, and this is an ounce. An ounce weighs twenty-eight grams," J.R. said, showing Devin how to use the digital scale.

"What's that?" Devin asked, pointing to the tanish-white squares on the kitchen counter.

"Bricks, birds, whole thangs, or squares. It's thirty-six ounces of cocaine, but when you cook it up like that…" Black pointed to the hard-white cookie looking chunks that Taco had just dumped onto the table. "By cooking the powder like Taco is doing, you can turn thirty-six ounces or whatever amount into more dope by rocking it up. You get a bigger profit, and more money; like these twenty packs of rocks that I chopped one gram of crack into seven twenty pieces. I can make more than just a hundred dollars off one gram. I make one hundred fifty dollars instead." Black said to the curious Devin, because black could remember back when he was that curious kid in the hood.

"Hey Devin, you ready to go to the club and hoop? It's already four o'clock," Jazz asked from the living room.

"Here I come!" Devin answered. "Yo we are about to bounce," Devin said to J.R., Taco, and Black.

"Come check on us tomorrow and see if we need y'all for something, ok?" Taco said, as he was letting the boys out the back door.

"How much money you got now?" Devin asked Vincent, as they walked through the projects, headed to the Boys Club.

"About sixty something."

"Yeah, that's about what I have too," said Devin.

"Devin ain't that your mom getting off the bus?" Jazz pointed.

"Oh shit!" Devin said, ducking behind a parked car. "If she seen me, I'm going to get killed when I get home."

"Don't trip! We can take the alley way by Conestoga school; she won't see us. Oh shit! Here she comes!" Vincent said jokingly, as they took off running down the alley laughing.

None of the boys knew that today would be the day that they would lose sight of their childhood dreams. No longer would their dreams be of being pro athletes. After today, because of the information their young ears and eyes should never have been privy to, but were, their lives would take a different path.

Chapter 3

After a long exhausting day of walking, swimming, and basketball, Devin, Vincent, and Jazz where rushing to get dressed after showering.

The Boys Club was only blocks from their homes, but they all had 9:00 pm curfews, because that was the time the Boys Club closed.

"Hurry up y'all, it's 8:45 pm," said Devin.

"I'm ready. Yo hurry up Jazz, if you want us to walk your scary ass halfway," said Vincent.

"Here I come!" Jazz said, still putting on his shirt as he caught up with Vincent and Devin.

It was dark and cold outside, and Devin couldn't wait to get home to see what his mom had cooked.

"I'll holla at y'all tomorrow don't let Booty Freaky Freddy get y'all," Jazz said laughing, as he started running through the empty lots toward his house.

For years there had been a story of a bootie bandit that would rape little boys in the North Omaha area. Most of the kids thought it to be just a story to scare kids. Little did they know Bootie Freaky Freddy was a real predator, and an everyday nightmare to his past victims.

"See you tomorrow V," Devin said, digging in the flowerpot to get his door key, watching Vincent walk down the street into the projects.

When Devin opened the front door the loud chronic smell of marijuana and his mom talking on the phone caught his attention and Devin stopped at the door.

"Girl I don't know what I am going to do. I was laid off work today and on top of me losing my job, they are cutting jobless benefits left and right. It's hard to pay these bills by myself as it is already. I don't know what I am going to do." Devin's mom said, as tears started to roll down her face.

Click! Devin tried to quietly shut the door when he heard the phone hang up. Feeling his mom's pain, Devin knew exactly what he was going to do, and no one could stop him.

The severity of the wrong choices and decisions Devin was about to make couldn't be stressed enough and his mind was made up. It was time to jump off the porch. He had to help his mom. They couldn't count on his dad to come back and save them. He had been gone since Devin was one.

"Fuck him, I got us," Devin said to himself, as he tried to sneak up the stairs.

"Devin is that you?"

"Damn!" Devin said under his breath. "Yeah, it's me Mom. Devin continued up the stairs to his room. Food was no longer on his mind. All he could think about now was everything he had seen, heard, and learned today from J.R., Taco, and Black, and how he could use that to help him and his mom. *Let me call my hitta*, Devin thought to himself, as soon as he heard his mom hang up the phone.

Rrring! Rrring! Rrring!

"Hello! Who in the hell is this?" Ms. Harris barked into the phone when she answered. She sounded mad at the world.

"Hi Ms. Harris. Is Vincent home?"

"Vincent! Vincent! Pick up the damn phone." Ms. Harris screamed in Devin's ear.

"Hello!"

"Hurry you ass up I need to use my phone!" Ms. Harris said, before slamming the phone down on the cradle.

"Damn your mom is mean as hell."

"Don't pay her no attention. What's up my hitta?" Asked Vincent?

"It's time to start making some real money. That's what's up!"

"How we gonna do that?"

"Like Taco and them!" Devin said, before he was interrupted by his mom.

"Devin, why you didn't come say hi Mom or something before you brought your narrow ass up to this room?" Devin's mom stood in the doorway with her hands on her hips.

"Hold on V," Devin said, before covering up the phone with his palm. "Sorry Mom, you was on the phone. How was your day?"

"Whateva boy and how many times have I told you about that sorry shit? It's not I'm sorry it's I apologize. I didn't raise no sorry kids. So, quit saying you are sorry and hurry up and get off that phone so you can eat. I made your favorite; fried chicken, mashed potatoes, and broccoli and cheese."

"Ok! Thanks Mom, you're the best." Devin said, placing the phone back to his ear. "Hello!"

"Thanks Mom, you the best." Vincent repeated Devin, jokingly.

"Whateva fool, you ready to get this money or what?"

"I'm with you 100% my hitta, but I doubt Taco will put us on."

"Let me handle that!" exclaimed Devin, turning up the volume on his TV, and turning to the channel 3 news."

Channel 3 Breaking News: Robbery suspect shot and killed by Omaha police today. The last of three men wanted in a kidnapping and robbery seven months ago was cornered in an abandoned building on 16th and Lake Street, when the suspect opened fire on Omaha police officers, shooting two of them. One officer died at the scene and the other is in critical condition. The robbery suspect, Tremain Davis, was gunned down and killed by Omaha police officers.

Davis of the 2400 unit of the Logan Fontenelle Housing Projects and two others, are accused of kidnapping a mother and daughter from a North Omaha small business and forcing them at gunpoint to open a home safe in West Omaha.

"Damn, that was Tray," said Vincent.

"I knew he was looking crazy. I can't believe he went out like that," Devin replied.

"Yeah, I knew something was up too, but I…"

"Vincent get off my damn phone!" Ms. Harris interrupted the line.

"Yo! I'll talk to you tomorrow," Vincent said.

"One." Devin said, hanging up the phone.

Chapter 4

It was late when Devin finished eating dinner. His mom had already gone up to bed, and even though Devin was tired and needed to get some sleep before school the next day, he could not sleep. All he could think about was getting money, and what it would be like if his dad was there to help them. Devin imagined how different life would be, if he had a dad at home. His young mind was in overdrive, as he drifted to sleep.

Boom! Boom! Boom! Boom! Boom! Boom! Loud gunshots rang out, as if they were in the house shooting. Startled out of his sleep by the loud gun shots, Devin rolled from his bed to the floor. The gunshots seemed to last for hours, even though it was only about a minute.

"Devin! Devin! Are you ok Baby?" Devin's mom asked, worried as she ran into her son's room and noticed him on the floor.

"It's ok Mom, get down!"

"No, it's not ok. I am so tired of this shit. This neighborhood, them projects, and gunshots every night, this shit is driving me crazy." Devin's mom said, as they laid on the floor.

"Everything's going to be ok Mom." Devin responded minutes after the gunshots had stopped, helping his mom up off the floor and to her room, promising her that he would get them out of this hell hole.

The rest of the night Devin laid in bed thinking about making lots of money and getting his mom out of the ghetto. Before he knew it, he was sound asleep.

Norris Jr. High School, located on the southwest side of town, was the school Devin and his friends attended. Like most of the kids in the

North Omaha area, they were bused to schools outside of their neighborhoods. There was a bus stop on the corner of the block Devin lived on, and another in the middle of the projects where Vincent, Chuck, Jamarl, and some of the other kids from the projects got on the bus. On days that Devin or some of the other kids that lived in the houses close to the projects missed their bus, they would run into the projects and try to catch it there before it pulled off. Today Devin had gotten to the bus stop on time, but school was the furthest thing from his mind.

"What's up with you D?" Vincent asked, as he pounced down on the seat in front of Devin's.

"What's up V?"

"What's good D?" Asked the tall and lanky Chuck.

"Same shit, different toilet," answered Devin. "Where's Jamarl?"

"Yo shit is crazy in the hood D. Last night two cars came through the hood blasting some crazy desert storm type of shit. I ain't never heard shots like that," said Vincent.

"Yeah, that shit sounded crazy. I heard it too. It sounded like it was in my front yard," said Devin.

"They smoked Chris last night," Chuck sadly said.

"Jamarl's brother Chris?" Asked Devin.

"Yeah! And another one of the homies, but what's really fucked up is they still got their bodies laying out on the cold ground this morning for everybody to see, while they take pictures acting like they trying to solve what happened. I've seen more bodies than the morgue, but not once have I seen on the news, murder case in the projects solved," barked Vincent.

"Yellow tape everywhere! It's fucked up that the first thing you see when you come out your home in the morning for school, is someone you know laying on the ground dead. It's gonna be some get back!" Chuck boldly exclaimed.

"I'm gonna definitely ride for the big homie," said Vincent.

When the bus turned into the school parking lot, none of their minds were on school.

"Yo! I'm not with this school shit this morning," Devin said.

"Me neither, but we are already here," added Chuck.

"So, let's leave. The teachers act like they don't want to teach us anyway. It's not like they are gonna miss us. We can take the city bus back to the hood," Devin said.

"That's what's up. I'm with that," said Chuck.

"Y'all not leaving me in this boring ass school. Let's go!" Vincent said, as the crew exited the bus, and headed to the back of the school instead of going inside like the rest of the students.

∞ ∞ ∞ ∞ ∞ ∞ ∞ ∞ ∞

This morning was dragging along slowly for Jazz. School was not the same without his crew. No one in the crew had perfect attendance, but all of them missing on the same day, something just wasn't right about it. Jazz had walked the halls from Chuck and Vincent's lockers, all the way around to Devin's locker; still nothing, not one of them to be seen. He was on his way to class when he spotted Keisha and her girlfriends in the hall.

Keisha was a fine young chocolate dime piece, from the same projects as Chuck and Vincent. Jazz had always had a crush on her. They were the same age, but the way she carried herself and by her looks, you would think she was a junior in high school. Today Keisha had on a pair of skintight Baby Phat jeans that hugged her milk shake thick thighs and hips and her small Baby Phat shirt made her breasts look perfect on

27

her frame. Her long silky hair with her chocolate complexion made her look like a model.

"What's up Keish?" Asked Jazz.

"Hello Jazz, where's the rest of the crew?"

"That's what I was gonna ask you. I guess they didn't want to come to school today."

"You are tripping, I seen all of 'em except Jamarl this morning on the bus."

"You sure? I've been looking all over this school for them."

"I don't know what to tell you. All I know is that they were on the bus this morning."

Rrrrringgg! The class bell rang.

"Damn Jazz! You got me late for class."

"My bad Keish, holla at cha later," said Jazz. *Something's not right. They were on the bus, but I can't find them anywhere. What is going on?* Thought Jazz, heading into his classroom.

Chapter 5

When the boys finally reached the projects, they were exhausted from the long city bus ride, from the southside of town to the northside. Crack Alley was business as usual. The dope fiends were out looking to score that early morning hit of crack or whatever their drug of choice, and the hustlers were more than willing to serve them their poison.

Crack Alley was a breeding ground for hustlers, and a death trap for the weak and lame minded. It was like a carnival, a rest haven for criminals. Any violation of the law one could think of happened here almost every day from murder, to robbery, assault, gambling, prostitution, and drug sales. There were so many different characters and things, it was like a city within a city; always something going on and this morning was no different. Fiends would come from all parts of the state to buy crack and coke, and whoever had the best product, made the most money. There have been so many dreams and lives lost in Crack Alley, that they were nicknamed 'Little Vietnam Projects.' Today Devin would be made a soldier in the game; unbeknownst.

Instead of playing catch and being taught things from his father like a normal thirteen-year-old boy, Devin would learn the morals, principals, and rules of the street. The ghetto had claimed another fatherless child into a very cold game.

∞ ∞ ∞ ∞ ∞ ∞ ∞ ∞ ∞

As the boys walked through Crack Alley some of the hustlers asked why they were not in school. Chuck stopped to talk to some of the older boys that he hung out with, that were either playing hooky also from school, or they had already dropped out. Vincent was headed over to Jamarl's, but there was only one thing on Devin's mind, and that was meeting up with Taco, Black and J.R.

"Yo D! Where you headed homie?" Vincent called, from Jamarl's porch.

"I'll be over in a minute. I'm gonna go handle this business for us first," Devin said, as he continued on his mission, his only reason for skipping school in the first place. He was almost to his destination when he heard the most sickening scream of pain, a terrifying loud yelp, and then Mr. Howard crashing out the door right in Devin's path. He made it about five steps, and then collapsed on the sidewalk in front of Devin. A long butcher's knife was sticking out his neck, and blood was spraying his shirt crimson, spattering all over the ground.

Mr. Howard flipped on the ground like a fish out of water, blood bubbles coming from his neck, as he stared up at Devin with cold eyes and wheezed his last breath like he wanted to say something. It was all over, Mr. Howard was dead, never would he put his hands on his wife again. Devin could not believe what he had just seen. He stood there in shock; just staring. This was the first time he had ever witnessed someone dying.

"I told him not to hit me anymore. Look what you made me do." Mrs. Howard stumbled out the house screaming and crying, throwing herself on top of Mr. Howard. "Please don't leave me Baby. I love you!"

Devin had seen enough and took off running as fast as he could, as if he was in a race, and he did not stop until he reached his destination.

Young Money

Bang…Bang…Clank! Devin banged on the screen door repeatedly, while looking behind him as if someone was chasing him. When the door opened Devin just walked in. He didn't even notice who had opened the door until he turned around and locked eyes on the baddest girl he had ever seen. Her caramel skin looked so soft and her nipples were poking through her wife beater like rockets. The print on the front of her too tight boy shorts was crazy fat. She was thick in all the right places.

"Um… What? Can I help you?" She asked with attitude, snapping Devin out of his trance.

"Oh, my bad!" Devin said, peeling his eyes off the girl's ass cheeks that were hanging out the bottom of her shorts. "Is Taco here?"

"Taco! Somebody's down here for you," she yelled up the stairs.

Taco came down the stairs in a wife beater and Roca Wear shorts. "What's up D? Why you not in school?" Asked Taco, slapping the beautiful girl on the ass, as she walked upstairs.

"I needed to get at you like ASAP," Devin said, watching each of the girl's ass cheeks rise then fall, as she walked up the stairs.

"What's up Little Homie? How can I help you?"

"I need you to put me on. It's all bad at my house. My mom just got fired from her job, I'm tired of wearing this bullshit ass gear, and I don't want my mom to have to go ask some man for money to help pay her bills. I'm tired of that shit Big Homie."

"What's up with your dad?"

"I don't have a dad. At least I've never met him."

"Damn! That's fucked up."

"What's up Taco? I am ready to get this money. Don't trip on my age. I got this. I…"

"Hold up, slow down," Taco said, cutting Devin off. "I got you Little Homie. This is what we are gonna do. Here's two hundred dollars. I have to fly back home today to take care of some business and I need you to hold some stuff down for me until I get back. Can you handle that?"

"I got you Big Homie, no doubt!" Devin responded, smiling from ear to ear.

"Do you know where 29th and Spaulding is?" Taco asked, running from the back room to look out the window, as the sound of sirens got closer. "Damn! I wonder what's going on now. The police and ambulance are across the way"

Devin was so caught up with his business with Taco, that he almost forgot about Mrs. Howard killing her husband. "Mrs. Howard killed her husband." Devin said, as if it was nothing, while he looked out the window at the crowd that was now forming to see what was going on.

"What?" Damn these are some wild projects. Motha fuckas stay getting murked around here." Taco said, closing the curtains back. "So, do you know where 29th and Spaulding is?"

"Yeah! I know where it's at."

"I need you to take these two birds to J.R. and Black. It's two and a half birds and a 4 - nickel in this other bag. Put it up somewhere safe and hold it for me until I get back."

"I got you Big Homie."

"You got a phone at home?"

"Yeah!"

"What's the number and please hold my shit down. I would hate to kill your young ass," Taco said sternly.

Devin gave Taco his phone number then placed the two birds for J.R. and Black into the backpack, with the rest of the stuff.

"Hold on let me write the address and Black's cell phone number down for you, then I'll call you a taxi."

"I'm cool. I will call a ride from my house. I gotta go get my hitta and put your stuff up first," Devin said, getting the paper with the address and phone number on it.

"Tell Black to call me when you get there."

Devin pulled the backpack over his shoulders and started on his journey. While walking, he passed the crime scene and Mrs. Howard sitting in the back of a police cruiser staring out the window at him with the same cold eyes as Mr. Howard. She looked so lost that Devin felt sorry for her.

The crowd was beginning to thin out. That's when Devin noticed Vincent.

"Where you been D? Mrs. Howard killed Mr. Howard," Vincent said, as if it was nothing.

"I know, I seen it when it first happened," Devin said, in a low tone so no one else could hear.

"What cha mean you know you seen it?"

"Come on I'll tell you all about it, while we take care of this business."

"Business? What's in the backpack? Where we going?"

"Damn! Come on twenty-one questions, just follow me. We gotta stop by my house and call a ride."

"A ride! A ride where?"

"Just come on fool, damn!"

Chapter 6

After hiding the gun and the two and a half birds of cocaine at his house, Devin and Vincent started on their mission to deliver what was left in the backpack. Vincent had no idea what was in the backpack, where they were going, or that Devin had hidden the two and a half birds and a 4-5 in the attic. Vincent was just enjoying his day. But for Devin, it was his first mission in the game, and he was feeling proud to be making some real money, not that chump change bottle money.

The boy's rode in the jitney cab in silence down 24th Street, until they reached the Lake Street overpass. Devin passed Vincent one of the two one hundred dollar bills that Taco had given him.

"We in the game now. We gonna get this money fo' real."

"Damn! Taco put you on?" Vincent whispered.

"I told you last night we gonna get this money. I got us V." Devin said, focused and excited to be doing a delivery for Taco. He was in the game now, and there was no turning back. He would do what he did best just like in school; observe and absorb until he knew everything. Just like he worked his way to the head of his class, he was now focused to do the same in the dope game. He had that drive, and the streets were about to find out.

"Yo V! You thirsty? I am. Hey driver stop at Dailey's store for me."

The cab driver had no problem pulling over at Dailey's. Devin had already paid-up front, plus he gave a nice tip.

"Stay in the cab V, I don't want this fool to leave us right here." Devin said, getting out of the cab to go inside. Devin still had the backpack on.

As Devin was coming out of the Dailey's with two bottles of orange Sunkist sodas and two bags of lays bar-b-que chips, a fiend approached him.

"You holdin? Let me get a $50. I got $45," the man said, shifting his weight from side to side.

"I'm not holding right now, but I got that fire you gonna be right here?" Devin asked the skinny talkative man.

"No, but I live across the street in the Spencer's." The Spencer Projects were a much smaller housing project on 30th Street, across from Dailey's. "They call me Bo-Bo. My spot is 2944 whenever you get on come through. If you got some good dope my spot rolls."

"That's what's up. I'll holla at you in a minute," Devin replied, climbing back into the jitney.

"Mr. Dailey been getting that money for a long time," Vincent said, opening his soda.

"Fo' sho! He even owns that bar Stage II across the street." Devin pointed.

"I seen him drop that boy Tedd's mom off in the hood the other day in a clean ass corvette. But check it, why did you tell that dope fiend you had some dope?"

"Because we are about to be on. I told you I ain't playing that's my word; as soon as we get to where we are going and drop this bag full of dope off."

"Damn! I knew you was up to something!"

"When I went to see Taco this morning, that's how I knew Mr. Howard got killed. I seen that shit. Ugh… I will never forget it either. I watched him die V. The shit was crazy homie. Yo! I think this is the house."

"Yeah, this is it," Vincent said, looking at the paper with the address on it.

"Y'all need me to wait?" The cab driver asked, as they climbed out the back.

"Nah, we will call the 30th and Bedford number when we get ready. "We might be here for a little while."

"Here's my card. Just call me whenever you need a ride."

"Fo' sho!" Devin grabbed the jitney driver's card, then him and Vincent slowly made their way up the sidewalk to the house and knocked.

"Who dat?" A voice yelled from inside the house.

"Lil D!"

"What's up Little Homie?" Black said, standing to the side of the now opened door. Weed smoke was strong in the air, as Devin and Vincent made their way inside the clean and well decorated house.

"Where's J.R.?" Asked Devin.

"His horny ass is upstairs." And as if on cue, you could hear moans and the bed squeaking.

"Here you go." Devin pulled the backpack from over his shoulders and gave it to Black.

"Thanks, Little Homie. Taco told me you were coming. Here's the two hundred dollars he said I owe you," Black said, peeling two one hundred-dollar bills from a large roll of money he pulled out of the pocket of his Sean John jeans.

"Now that's what I'm talking about!" Devin said joyously, giving Vincent one of the hundred-dollar bills.

"Good lookin out my hitta." Vincent was all smiles, impressed by the move Devin had put together.

"Don't trip. I'm gonna make sure we are straight from here on out," Devin said, giving Vincent a fist pound.

"So, what are you two about to get into?" Asked Black.

"I was wondering if I could get some work from you. I got some money."

"You think you ready to get this d-boy money huh?"

"I know I'm ready Big Homie."

"Don't get caught up in the hype, the cars, clothes, money, and all the nice things, because this is really a cold game Little Homie. It's not for the weak, Lil D."

"I ain't weak!" Devin muttered.

"I know you not. I just wanted you to know that this dope game is real. This ain't a movie Homie. Motha fuckas get killed over this shit. It's some fucked up people in this game, from the hustlers you deal with, to the fiends you serve. You have to be about that mess, no punks allowed, and you gotta stay focused."

"I hear you loud and clear Big Homie, but where we are from," Devin gave Vincent a pound again. "We are born about that life. Ain't no punks here. We just need somebody to give us the game and put us on!"

"This is what I'm gonna do," Black smiled, impressed with the young go getters attitude. "Lil D, I knew you were ready that day I met you. I seen how you was watching us. But you know it takes money to make money, right?"

"How much money you got on you V?" Devin asked Vincent, before Black could even finish his sentence.

"You didn't let me finish, this first one is on me. I'm gonna do y'all like my big homie did me. I'm gonna put this work together and show you the whip game. Whatever is left over in crumbs and pieces on the towel when we get done bagging it up, y'all can have it."

"That's what's up!" Devin said, not really knowing what Black was talking about. He just knew they were gonna be given some work.

I didn't know we had company! What's up D? What's up V?" J.R. said, noticing Devin and Vincent, when he came downstairs with a bad yellow bone with green eyes. As she walked, it was like she was modeling the apple bottom jeans that looked painted on her fat ass. Her shirt was tied in the front, showing off her flat stomach and small waist. The girl was island fine, looking like a thick young Lisa Ray. Devin and Vincent couldn't keep their eyes off her.

"Man, I'm hungry. Y'all hungry?" J.R. asked but didn't wait for a response, before telling the beautiful girl to go get them something to eat.

"Eugh! You know I gotta get back to work. I'm only going to Time Out, since it's around the corner."

"That's cool! I heard they got the best fried chicken in the Midwest. Get us a box of chicken, some fries, and some sodas," J.R. said, giving her some money.

"I'm gonna call when I am outside, and don't forget you are gonna get my hair did for sweating it out," the Redbone said, strolling out the door.

"Yo! You done playing porno star Mr. Marcus? We got work to put together," Black said jokingly.

"This the work?" J.R. asked, grabbing the backpack off the table and heading towards the kitchen. "So, what's up with y'all, Little Homies?"

"They ready for you to put that work together for them, so they can get their hustle on," Black said. "I told them we would put them on and give 'em the game."

"Oh yeah! Y'all ready?" J.R. asked from the doorway of the kitchen. "Welcome to the family. Come on in here and let me give you the game on how to put this dope together. Don't trip, it's free this time, but the whip game costs."

Devin and Vincent gave Black and J.R. their full attention, soaking up all the game that was being given to them. Devin was very meticulous and after the first batch of dope that J.R. cooked, there was no doubt in Devin's young mind, that he could cook dope into crack.

Beep. Beep. Beep. Beep.

"Yo Devin! Go get that food, so her crazy ass will quit blowing that horn," J.R. said, not taking his eyes off what he was doing.

When Devin got to the car, it was like he was being hypnotized when he looked into the girl's pretty green eyes.

"Say cutie, tell J.R. not to forget to call me before he leaves." The girl said, before speeding off in her convertible Sebring.

When Devin returned back to the kitchen with the food, there were already hard white blocks of crack on the table cooling on a towel.

"That didn't take long!"

"Don't' take long with this straight drop A-1 yola," Black said, already at the table with a razor and scale.

"When you see the dope start to gel like this, that's when you use your wrists like this to bring it all together." J.R. continued to school Devin, who stared at the clear Pyrex pot with intentness. "Then it's time for some cold water or ice." J.R. said, moving to the sink to drain the water before placing more large blocks of crack on the towel in front of Black and Vincent. "And be sure that you never put the wrap that your dope came in, in your garbage that you send to the curb. Dump that shit somewhere else. You don't need motha fuckas stumbling up in your business."

After Black finished bagging for him and J.R., there was a lot of chunks, pieces, and crack shavings still left over on the towel.

"Y'all can have the rest of this dope on the towel," Black said, grabbing a piece of chicken out of the box and biting into it. "Damn! This chicken in good!"

Devin and Vincent were excited looking at all the crack left over on the towel.

"Hey! Black will this gel back if I cook it again?" Devin asked, curiously.

Impressed, Black and J.R. stared at each other and smiled. "Yeah! That's a good idea. Go ahead do your thing," replied Black.

Vincent watched, as Devin dumped all the crack that was on the towel into a large Pyrex cup, and then copied everything that he had seen J.R. do, step by step. All eyes were on Devin, as all the shavings, crumbs, and pieces started to gel.

"No, he didn't?" Black said, astonished, watching Devin pull the Pyrex cup out of the larger pot of boiling water.

"He might whip better than you Black," J.R. said, as he watched Devin with the potholders on his hands, twirl the cup side to side and round and round, until everything inside is locked up.

"Wa-la!" Devin said, when he had finished and dumped the contents of the cup onto the towel.

"Damn! The boy is a natural. Taco said he trusted they were ready, but wait until I tell him about this," Black said to J.R.

"That's my hitta!" Vincent was excited, as he placed the boulders of crack onto the scale. "Sixty-two grams."

"Hey Black!" J.R. called, as Black walked into another room. "Can you believe he got two and a quarter back off the towel?"

"Pass me one of those razors V and bust that shit down 31 – 31."

"We on now! Here you go D." Vincent gave Devin thirty-one grams and then started chopping his dope into twenty-dollar pieces of crack. "Black! This good for twenty dollars?"

"Use your scale like I showed you and remember, one gram is a hundred dollars. Try to get at least six or seven twenty pieces out of a gram," said Black. "The game is about making a good profit off what you spend, a quick flip of your money."

"We got it for free, but I want every dime out of mine," Devin said, cutting his dope with the razor.

It was close to 3:00 pm when Vincent and Devin finished weighing, chopping, and bagging their dope.

"V, you ready?" Asked Devin.

"Yeah, let's get this money. I can't wait to get back to the hood."

"Y'all need to call a ride?"

"Yeah, we got the driver's number that dropped us off."

"Shit, you might as well give them those new mountain bikes. You're not gonna ride 'em."

"How you know I'm not gonna ride them?" Asked Black.

"Because yo fat ass ain't gonna be here." J.R said. "I don't know why you bought them in the first place."

"A piece of crack for two brand new mountain bikes why not? Yo! Y'all want these mountain bikes?"

"I want the red one," Vincent replied.

"It don't matter which one, they both look expensive to me," Devin said, looking at the nice bikes. "What do we owe you for 'em Black?"

"That's small shit, y'all family now, you don't owe me shit. Just remember death before dishonor," Black said sternly.

"Call us tomorrow, because we might be leaving in a couple days," said J.R.

"And be safe!" Black said, as the boys rolled their new bikes out the front door.

"Good looking out y'all," Devin said, already on his new bike.

"I can't wait to get back to the hood," Vincent said, getting on his bike.

"I want to step in the Spencer's and holla at old dude I was talking to at Daileys." Devin said. "It's on the way."

"We don't know that fool D! He could be trying to set us up."

"Then we gonna be the last motha fuckas he set up." Devin exposed the gun on his waist to Vincent, by pulling his t-shirt up, so he could see the 4–5.

"Ewww! I want one." Vincent said, like Devin had a new toy.

Young Money

"Taco gave it to me to put up for him, but I didn't want to get caught slippin. We in the game now so we gotta stay strapped." Devin said, feeling the power because he was strapped.

Chapter 7

When Devin and Vincent arrived in the Spencer Projects, it looked like a dope fiend anniversary in front of the address Bo-Bo had given Devin.

"Y'all seen Bo-Bo?" Devin asked, with one foot on the ground and one on the pedal.

"Why? Who you?"

"Friends of Bo's." Vincent responded.

"Y'all got some work?" Asked one of the fiends.

"Come on Baby, I think he's in the house," the female standing outside said, trying her best to appear sexy. She looked like she had lost that sexy a long time ago, along with her teeth and weight. You couldn't tell her that though, because she was in full denial. "Bo, you got company. Come on in, he's here somewhere."

The living room was dark. Only the sun coming through the slits of the soiled curtains provided light, along with the old outdated floor model tv with the rolling fuzz lines, that would cause eye problems if you dared to look at the picture too long. There was a dingy sofa with white cushions, trying to escape through the many holes in the sofa. The wallpaper was peeling too. Also, there was a strong unfamiliar odor in the air, mixed with the incense that was sticking out of the wall burning, leaving ashes on the already soiled floor.

"What's up Lil D?" I didn't think you was coming through. It's been rolling, but ain't nothing but some bullshit dope around here. Motha fuckas don't want that shit. You ain't got that bullshit, do you?"

44

"Nah, we got that A-1!" Devin said proudly.

"Here, I got ten dollars. Let me get a nice piece to try out, and I will work off the rest if it's good." Bo said fidgety.

"What 'cha mean work off the rest?" Asked Devin.

"You take care of me and I will bring all the customers to you. You can set up shop in here."

"That's what's up. Give me the ten dollars." Devin turned his back to Bo to pull a twenty piece out of his sack.

It seemed like Bo gave Devin the money, got his crack, and was firing up his pipe all at the same time.

"Ooh...ooh!" Bo smacked his lips like he was tasting food. "Eughwee...ummm...hmmm!" He smiled, with his lips still on the pipe then passed it to the woman who had escorted them in. She had been intensely watching Bo hit the pipe.

She hit the pipe one hard time, closed her eyes, and started smacking her lips. "Here Baby, hook me up," she said in her sexy voice, pulling twenty dollars from between her sagging breasts.

Devin gave her a twenty piece, then called for Vincent to bring the bikes in.

"Bo it's some people outside looking for you." Vincent turned his nose up because of the pungent odor in the room.

"Customers!" Bo said, with high-beamed eyes. He gave the woman the pipe back, then disappeared outside. When he came back, he was with two men.

"I heard you got that heat," the tall man with the old school afro said. "Let me get a fifty."

Devin took three pieces from his bag, then chipped one in a half pieces with his fingernails. "Here you go Old School." Devin said, showing the man the crack in the palm of his hand.

"Good looking out!" The man said, giving Devin the fifty dollars when he saw Devin wasn't gonna give him the work in his hands, until he passed him the money.

"I got thirty dollars. Hook me up," the other man said. "I'll be back to spend, if it's that heat like Bo said."

Devin gave the man a piece out of his bag with the piece he had chipped off.

"Alright my man, you gonna be posted here?"

"Yeah! This my dude, he will definitely be posted here," Bo said, putting his arm around Devin's shoulder.

"That's what's up, good looking out Bo," the men said, then exited Bo's front door.

"Yo Bo! I gotta bounce," Devin said, noticing what time it was. He knew that his mom would be at home, because she had lost her job.

"What! Why you leaving? It's about to start rolling fo' real around here after 5:00 pm."

"Don't trip, I'll be back in an hour. I got something I have to take care of," Devin said, giving Bo a piece of crack, before him and Vincent left.

"Y'all holding?" A fiend approached Devin and Vincent before they could get on their bikes.

"What 'cha need?" Vincent asked.

"Let me get a..." The man uncrumbled the bills from his pockets. "I got thirty-seven dollars."

Vincent pulled two pieces from his bag, grabbed the money from the man, then gave him the crack.

The man tasted the dope with his tongue, said thanks, then walked off.

"Man, why we leaving D?" Asked Vincent.

"My mom is gonna start bugging out if I don't come home right after school, so I'm gonna go check in, then say I'm going to the club. You can stay if you want, I'm coming back. You can keep the strap."

"Nah I'm good. I told Jamarl and Chuck that I would kick it with them."

"Damn! I forgot about Jamarl. How is he holding up?"

"He's just trying to stay strong for his mom, but he's talking about putting in some work with the homies, to get some get back."

"Be careful Homie!"

"Nah, you be careful when you go back to the Spencer's." Vincent said, as they parted to go their separate ways.

Devin thought he would have to answer all types of questions from his mom when he opened the door and walked in the house. To his surprise his mom wasn't home, but there was a note on the refrigerator.

Devin do not forget to take the trash to the curb. There is dinner from Skeets bar-b-que in the refrigerator. I have to work at the bar tonight, so I will be home late. Make sure my doors are locked when you go to the Boys Club. If you need me call me, you know the number to the bar. Love you son, and don't forget to leave the porch light on.

"Hell yeah! Green light!" Devin said, placing the bar-b-que in the microwave, then going out the back door to get the gun and crack he had stashed. After locking the door back, Devin placed the gun on the table, ate a couple pieces of the bar-b-que ribs, then tucked the gun in his belt under his shirt and headed back to Bo's, with the bag of crack stuffed down in his underwear.

∞ ∞ ∞ ∞ ∞ ∞ ∞ ∞ ∞

The Spencer Projects were alive and much more active then when Devin and Vincent were there earlier. Now there were kids playing hopscotch, little girls jumping rope, music blasting, girls braiding hair, a dice game on one of the porches, and a crowd of people posted up in Devin's path to Bo's.

All eyes were on Devin as he passed, at least that's what it felt like to him as he received a lot of crude stares, mean mugs, and ice grillz. This neighborhood was not in Devin's comfort zone. He was on alert, but not scared.

"Hey! Hey D! What took you so long?" Bo yelled, appearing out of the crowd. "I got people lined up at the house. I've been waiting for you, but I was about to cop from someone else."

"What's up Bo-Bo?" Asked the boy in a blue Dickie suit.

"Never mind now," Bo said to the guy who had just fell off on the dice game.

"What?" The guy gave Bo a cold stare, and Devin a once over from head to toe.

"I told you I was coming back," Devin said, keeping his composure.

"Come on!" Bo rushed Devin into the house with his bike.

"Bo, I'm about to go man. I am…"

"Yo, relax slim, this my man right here."

"Damn! How old are you boy?" Asked Slim.

"Don't nothing matter, but money, Slim. What 'cha trying to cop?" Devin asked, sternly.

"What can you do for these seventy-five dollars?" Slim asked.

"I got 'cha." Devin said, placing four pieces in his palm for Slim.

Slim looked at the dope in Devin's hands, then rushed into his pockets and gave him the money. "What's your name Lil Homie? How can I get up with you again?"

"They call me Lil D. Just holla at Bo, this is where I'm gonna be."

"I got fifty bucks, let me get a little love like that," said the other man that was in the living room when Devin entered.

Devin served all the people that were already in the house when he entered, and a couple more that came in after him. When the traffic finally died down, he broke Bo-Bo off a proper piece. Then Bo-Bo disappeared upstairs with what he called his strawberry, causing Devin to laugh because it was the prom fiend that he had met earlier.

A couple more fiends came, copped, and left before Bo-Bo came downstairs. Some bought crack to smoke in the house, but Devin could tell they really didn't want to stay and smoke there, because they had to share with Bo. However, some seemed to not care to share with Bo. Devin was amazed at how much Bo could smoke.

Nightfall had finally come, Bo disappeared outside somewhere, and the house was quiet. The tv had no sound and Devin was restless pacing the floor from the back to the front checking the locks, then he opened the front door and looked out.

The streetlights were on and most of the kids had been called into their homes. The crowd scattered throughout the small projects, having their own conversations and hustlin car to car and hand to hand.

Looking out, Devin noticed that the traffic had slowed down on the inside, but not the outside.

Curiously, Devin stepped out onto the small porch and watched the goings on like a movie. It wasn't like Crack Alley, but it was a drug strip all the same. 30th Street was busy with traffic, and Dailey's Liquor Store and Stage II across the street had lots full of cars and people.

"Flap!" The door opening and closing startled Devin to reach for his strap.

"What's up?" A short stocky kid, probably a little older than Devin said, as he sat down on the porch next to Devin.

"Just chillin, checking on the view and trying to get this money," Devin replied.

"He's looking right there. Yo! I got that bomb," yelled the stocky kid.

"I got twelve dollars," the fiend said, holding the crumbled bills in his shaking hands.

Devin reached into his pockets and broke off a piece with his two fingers, not wanting to pull all his dope out. The fiend gave Devin his money, then placed the dope he got from him into his mouth and walked away.

"How did you know he was looking to buy some dope?" Devin asked.

"It's easy! You just gotta be out here. I know the looks, the faces, the big eyes, and the way they move. I use to sit out here and watch my dad get money before he got killed. Him and your dad would sit out here just like this."

"My dad?"

"Yeah, him and Bo."

"Bo-Bo ain't my dad!"

"My bad. I thought Bo was your dad." The boys started laughing together.

"Nah, he's just helping me hustle."

"I knew you wasn't from around here, so I thought Bo was your dad or something."

"I'm from the Bottoms." Devin said proudly.

"Do you live by the Boys Club? We play them this Saturday at Kellom."

"Yeah, I live by the club. Who do you play for?"

"I play for the 9th Grade Adams team."

"I play for the club and all of our teams are undefeated, the 7th, 8th, and 9th grade teams."

"We haven't lost yet either. Which team do you play for?"

"I play on the 8th grade team," Devin said. "But I'm coming to watch the…"

"Yo Lil D, what's poppin?" Slim interrupted the two boys.

"What the business is Slim?" Devin questioned. This was the same man he met earlier, only now the man was sharply dressed in snakeskin from head to toe. Devin was tickled by his snakeskin suit and matching boots.

"Trying to get my hoes a blast, before I put them on the track." Slim pointed to a clean Cadillac full of women.

"What 'cha trying to spend Slim?"

"A dollar! Hook me up again. I'm gonna keep spending with you as long as the dope is good." Slim gave Devin a hundred-dollar bill.

"The dope is always gonna be A-1 coming from me. Let's go inside. I'll be back," Devin said to the kid from next door.

Slim watched with bulging eyes, as Devin pulled the sandwich bag full of crack from his pockets.

"Damn youngsta you got more dope than Scarface in your pockets. Be careful out here Lil D," Slim said, shaking his head in satisfaction with the five rocks Devin placed in his hands.

"I'm straight OG!" Devin exposed the 4-5 under his shirt.

"Damn that motha fucka is bigger than you." Slim laughed, then headed out the door.

"Devin who was that going out the door?" Bo asked, startling Devin because he didn't know that Bo had come in through the back door.

"Pimpin Slim," Devin said, walking back out the front.

"What you doing out here? Oh, what's up Chris?" Bo asked, noticing his next-door neighbor.

"Trying to get to the money. It slowed down so I came outside when you left," Devin answered.

"Got that bomb!" Little Chris waived to the car that had slowed to a stop.

The nice car parked, and the woman on the passenger side got out and walked over to the porch. "Y'all got that good?"

"I got that A-1 Sexy, what 'cha trying to spend?" Devin asked, looking at the girl from head to toe. She did not have the looks of a fiend, she was too fine. Devin was so focused on the woman's body that he didn't notice the three guys in the cut at the end of the building watching his every move.

"Let me get a dub on a hundred."

"A dub on a hundred?" Devin asked confused.

"That's double on what you would give up on the regular. I think she's trying to get her hustle on." Lil Chris whispered to Devin.

Once Devin learned what a double up was, he didn't want to serve the girl, but he did anyway. He pulled out nine pieces and placed them in his palms so she could see. She looked at the dope, smiled, and gave Devin a hundred dollars. "Thanks cutie," she said, then turned and walked off like she was on Rip the Runway. Everybody on the porch stared until she got in the car.

"Devin you gotta be careful cause its dangerous shiesty motha fuckas out here. Hold on!" Bo walked off to a car that had pulled up and parked.

"Bo is telling you some good shit D. Motha fuckas will kill you for a little of nothing on some jealous shit, plus you not from around here."

"I'm good Lil Chris." Devin patted his shirt where his gun was at.

"Oh shit! You strapped?" Asked a surprised Chris.

"Here!" Bo passed Devin twenty dollars.

"What time is it?" Devin asked, then gave Bo a twenty piece.

"Hold on let me go see." Chris got up and walked in the house.

"Here's forty more dollars," Bo said, short of breath from jogging from another car.

"It's 9:30 pm!" Chris said, coming out of the house.

"Oh shit! My momma gonna kill me." Devin jumped from the porch to get his bike from the house.

"Where you going D? It's rollin out here," Bo asked confused.

"I was supposed to be home a long time ago," Devin replied, giving Bo two more twenty pieces.

"At least leave me something to keep the spot rollin. I'll have your money tomorrow when you get here." Bo tried his best to sound innocent, fiending.

Not knowing the mistake, he was making, Devin gave Bo five more pieces of crack.

"I'll get this off. I got you tomorrow," Bo said, with his eyes on high beam, looking at all the dope that Devin had just placed in his hands.

"I'll holla at you tomorrow Bo. Later Chris," Devin said, climbing on his bike.

"Tomorrow D!" Chris watched Devin ride away, like he was in a race.

Chapter 8

When Devin reached his house, he placed his bike in the backyard, hid his gun, then walked to the front. He could hear music playing so he knew his mom was up waiting on him. Devin opened the door expecting to see his mom sitting at the table, but instead he could hear a man's voice talking to her when he walked into the living room. She was sitting on the couch with a man he had never seen before.

"Sorry I'm late, practice got…"

"Devin this is Steve," his mom interrupted him. "Steve this is my baby, Devin."

"What's up Devin? I've heard a lot about you," the man said, with his hand out for a pound or shake. Whatever it was for, he wouldn't be getting it from Devin.

Devin looked at the man's hand, then back at his mom. "I'm tired Mom. I'm gonna grab something to eat, then head to bed," Devin said, with an attitude, turning to walk to the kitchen. He was surprised that his mom wasn't going off because he came home past curfew.

"Warm that bar-b-que up," Devin's mom yelled over the music.

Devin placed the rest of the bar-b-que from Skeets into the microwave, grabbed a soda out the fridge, chips out the cabinet, then decided to call Jamarl.

Ring! Ring! The phone rang a couple times before a female voice answered, "Hello!"

"Can I speak to Jamarl?"

"Hold on." Devin could hear her place the phone down and then a lot of people in the background, as she called for Jamarl.

"Hello!"

"What's up Jamarl?"

"What up D? I hear y'all gettin to the money now," Jamarl said, over the loud noise in the background.

"Damn, that fool V talk too much."

"You know he couldn't wait to shine. Him and Chuck just left. They said they were going over to the Alley."

"It sounds like your spot is full of people. That's fucked up what happened to your brother. Just know whatever you need I'm here for you."

"That's what's up D. Thanks Homie. I really miss him already," Jamarl said, choking up, but doing his best to stay strong. "Yo, I'm gonna go catch up with Chuck and Vincent. I'll see you tomorrow. I gotta get out of this house, it's too much crying going on in here. I need some air," Jamarl explained.

"That's what's up, stay strong Homie. One!" Devin hung up.

Devin finished his food then headed upstairs. Once he got to his room, he locked the door behind himself, and turned on his CD player. "Yeah, trap or die," came screaming through the speakers, before Devin could turn the volume down a little.

Devin emptied his pockets onto the bed, then started uncrumbling all the bills. "Let's get it." Devin rapped along with the music, sorting the bills in separate piles: ones, fives, tens, twenties, fifties, and hundreds. When he finished counting, he had made over seven hundred dollars.

Devin was so excited as he counted the money over and over again. He had never been in possession of so much money, and this was all his money. He unscrewed one of the speakers to hide his dope inside the stereo. Devin was happier than a kid on Christmas Day.

Knock! Knock!

Devin turned the music down. "Mom," Devin said, opening the door to his room.

"I'm about to go to your Aunt Ann's. Her and your uncle Ron got into it again."

"They are always fighting. Hold on Mom, I'm going with you."

"Hurry up boy." Devin's mom turned to go back downstairs.

Devin's Aunt stayed on 29th and Pinkney, two blocks from the Spencer Projects, so Devin grabbed his crack sack, then ran down to the car.

When they reached his aunt's house, she was already outside waiting, cursing, and screaming, "Take me to get my car. He left in my damn car!"

"Devin go in the house until we come back," Devin's mom said.

That was music to Devin's ears, because now he could run over to the Spencer Projects. First, he had to let his cousin Herb know, so he went inside the house.

"What's up relative?" Herb said, taking the phone from his ear.

"Yo! I'll be right back."

"What! Where the fuck you going this late at night?"

"I got this little redbone that lives in the Spencer's and her mom is at work. I'll be right back," Devin said, walking out the door.

When Devin arrived in the Spencer Projects, he had to pass a couple of older guys standing in the dark cuts, hustling. They stared at Devin, but he paid them no attention.

This was Devin's first time in the projects late at night and without his gun. He didn't like the feeling, but he felt a little relieved when he got to Bo's house and the door was already open.

"Yo! Bo what's up? You in here? It's Lil D." Devin yelled through the house, but he received no answer back. He turned on some lights and just when he was about to sit down, there was a knock on the door.

"What the business is?" Devin asked the man standing on the porch.

"A thirty," said the man.

Devin took the money, and then placed the pieces of crack in the man's hand. When the man left, Devin locked the door behind him. Before he could sit down, there was another knock at the door. This time it was Bo's strawberry.

"What's up Cutie?" She said in her sexy tone. "Where's Bo at, is he here?" She asked, sounding a little nervous to Devin. He watched her look around with bugged out eyes.

"I don't know, why? What's up?" Devin asked, impatiently.

"Let me get a twenty, Boo."

Devin took her money, gave her a twenty piece of crack, then headed to the front door to let her out. When he turned, he could hear the backdoor closing. *Let me go lock this door,* he said to himself, heading to the back door. Just before Devin could reach the backdoor to lock it, three hooded men busted through with guns pointed at him.

"What th…"

"Get down or get laid down bitch!" One of the hooded men yelled, with his gun pointed in Devin's face.

Hesitant to get down, Devin tried to speak, "Wha…"

Smack! The cold steel of the hooded man's pistol was whipped with extreme force into Devin's face, splitting his lips and busting his nose.

"Aahhh!" Devin fell to the ground in agonizing pain, with blood dripping from his mouth and his nose.

"I'm only gonna ask you one time, where is the dope and money?" Asked one of the hooded men, before he violently kicked Devin in the side.

"Ummph." Devin tried to muffle the pain that shot up his body. When he tried to talk, he could taste his blood. It was at this moment, Devin's life started to flash before him. He just knew he was about to be killed, and he was so disappointed in himself for not bringing his gun.

"Pop his bitch ass!" Screamed one of the hooded men.

"The shit ain't worth dying for little niggah!"

"It's…It's in my pockets," Devin mumbled nervously.

One of the men aggressively started rummaging through Devin's pockets. That's when he got a glimpse of all their faces.

"Where's the rest of the shit at?" The man who appeared to be the leader asked, while putting the nose of his gun to Devin's head.

"Tha…tha…that's all I got." Devin could feel the cold hard steel pressed up against his head.

"I can't believe you got me on this bullshit ass mission," the man with the gun to Devin's head said to one of the other hooded men.

Devin closed his eyes, feeling that the man was about to pull the trigger, then he heard faint voices and the sound of keys at the front door. He wanted so badly to yell for help, but before he could muster the courage, he heard footsteps shuffling toward the back door.

"Huhhh!" Devin exhaled, glad to be alive, as he watched the hooded men fleeing out the backdoor.

"What the fuck?" Bo said, when he opened the door and noticed Devin lying on the floor bleeding. "What happened to you? What are you doing here? Are you ok?" Asked Bo, stretching his hand out for Devin, who was getting up off the ground.

"Hell nah, I'm not ok!" Devin exclaimed, wiping the blood from his face with his t-shirt. All I know is, I served your girlfriend, and when I went to let her out the front, she had already let herself out the back. Then, when I went to lock the door, motha fuckas rushed in with guns before I could get to it." Devin sounded shaken up.

"What? Are you shot?"

"Nah, motha fuckas busted me in the face with the pistol."

"Let me see your face," Bo said, examining. Those cuts and bruises fucked your nose up, but you will be ok. Let me get you a towel and some ice."

"I swear I'm gonna kill every last one of them motha fuckas Bo. They got me fucked up!" Devin exclaimed with hurt pride.

"Hold on Killa, put this on your face." Bo gave Devin a pack of ice wrapped in a towel. "I thought you said you wasn't coming back until tomorrow."

"I wasn't, but my mom had to drop me off over my aunt's house on 29th and Pinkney, so I walked back over here to see if it was still rolling. Devin could tell that his lips were swollen because they were affecting the way he talked. "I promise I will never be caught slippin again without my strap." He was angry and made a vow to himself, "I'm gonna kill them bitch ass niggahs."

Don't worry about it Lil D. I'm gonna find out who did this. I'm gonna find that crackhead bitch, and choke it out of her."

"You think she had something to do with it?" Devin asked confused.

"That crackhead bitch didn't have no money when I left, and she knows I don't let nobody go in or out my backdoor. Ima fuck that bitch up," Bo answered.

"I better head back to my aunt's house before they get back. I'll see you tomorrow Bo."

"Wait a couple days before you come back Lil D," Bo said, angry with himself for what had happened to the kid. Devin was too young to be going through this shit.

"Bo-Bo, you got me fucked up! Ain't nobody running me from my spot. This is where I get money and where I'm gonna keep getting money. Didn't you say this was my spot?" Devin barked at Bo.

"Whoa! Whoa! I'm on your side Lil D," Bo said, noticing the anger and fire in Devin, as he walked past him and out the door.

Devin was glad to see his mom and aunt had not made it back when he reached his aunt's house. It was an even bigger delight when his relative Herb opened the door and turned and went back to his room, without paying any attention to him.

When Devin's auntie walked into the house, Devin played like he was sleep. He had already done his best to clean himself up, but his mom still noticed when he reached the car.

"Boy what the fuck happened to you? Devin's mom looked him in the face.

"I bumped it on the corner of Aunt Ann's bathroom door. I wasn't paying attention when Herb was coming out the bathroom, and the door smacked me in the face." Devin told his mom a lie before climbing into the backseat.

When Devin got home, he was still steaming hot about what had happened. He couldn't sleep from thinking about getting robbed. He could have been killed, and that's all that was on his mind.

Chapter 9

The next morning, Devin woke up way before his alarm sounded. He was more than ready to get his day started. He had gotten a taste of money and had a big thirst for more, but first came school, so he checked his bruises in the mirror, then got dressed.

After getting himself together, Devin headed downstairs for some breakfast. When he reached the bathroom stairs, he was startled by a knock at the door. *Who could that be, this early?* He thought to himself, looking through the peephole.

"Jazz? What's up? What brings you this way so early my hitta?" Devin asked, letting Jazz in the house and closing the door.

"Devin who was that?" His mom asked, from the top of the stairs.

"Ain't nobody but Jazz Mom," Devin yelled back. "What's the business Jazz?" He asked.

"I was trying to figure out what was up with the crew. I didn't see none of y'all yesterday, and everybody I talked to at school said Jamarl was the only one not on the bus. That means y'all left and was up to something. Whateva it is, I won't miss out today," Jazz said.

"Boy you a fool! We skipped yesterday to take care of some business," Devin said, grabbing some pop tarts out the cabinet, before they left to catch the bus.

"What business?" Asked Jazz.

"Come on! I'll tell you about it." Devin hurried to the corner where the bus had pulled up.

"Whateva the business is, y'all better include me next time. It was boring as hell at school yesterday." Jazz questioned Devin non-stop all the way to the next stop.

"What's up Chuck? What's up Jamarl?" Devin was glad to see someone besides Jazz, who was really getting on his nerves. He hadn't stopped talking since he arrived at Devin's house.

"Same shit what's up with y'all? So, what brings you to our bus this morning Jazz?" Asked Chuck.

"Him felt like he was left out yesterday," Devin said, in a baby voice.

"Oh, you makin sure we don't leave you out today," Chuck laughed.

"Where's V at Chuck?" Devin asked.

"We bumped into a couple fiends on the way to the bus stop, so Vincent ran back to the house to get some dope to serve 'em."

"Gotta get that money!" Devin said.

"What happened to your face my hitta? Looks like you…?

"Oh shit! Yo yo Bus Driver stop the bus! You got one coming." Jazz yelled, when he noticed Vincent running out of the projects waving his hands in the air, trying to flag the bus down.

"I know yo rusty ass saw me coming," Vincent said to the bus driver, before he sat down in the seat winded. "What's up y'all? What's up Jazz?"

"Ain't nathen! I see you getting to the money," Devin said.

"Early bird gets the worm," Vincent responded, counting the crumbled bills in his lap.

"You serving now?" Jazz asked Vincent.

"We are all about to start getting this money. Ain't that right D?"

"Believe that!" Devin said, with a smile.

"Yeah right! Who gonna put us on?" Jazz asked curiously.

"Don't worry about that! Y'all down or what?" Vincent inquired.

"It's enough money for us, y'all trying to get down?" Devin asked, with a serious look on his face.

"I don't know the first thing about selling dope," Jazz said to his friends, as they walked into the cafeteria for breakfast.

"The dope sells itself, we getting that A-1 yola," Vincent replied, pulling out a stack of money to pay for his waffles.

"Aint no pressure, this shit ain't for everybody, plus you good anyway Jazz. But if you decide you want in, just holla at me. That goes for y'all too," Devin said to Jamarl and Chuck.

"You already know what's up with me. I'm trying to get some money," said Chuck.

"I will get with you after school," said Jamarl.

"I'm paying for us four," Devin told the cashier when they all arrived at the register.

"Well, you all have extra waffles, orange juice, and syrup!" The cashier said, with an attitude of doubt.

"I just asked for the total!" Devin exclaimed, pulling a large stack of money out of his pocket.

"Th…That will be $18.50," the cashier stuttered, surprised at the amount of money the young black kid held in his hands. *Probably stole it*, she thought to herself, receiving the twenty dollars from Devin.

"Thank you!" Devin said, receiving his change from the old grumpy white lady.

The boys sat at their normal table, and did their normal routine of eating talking, and checking out the baddest females, as they strutted into the cafeteria.

"Damn! These waffles are good!" Devin stuffed his mouth with more waffles.

"Yo! Check Keisha out in them tight ass jeans," Jamarl said.

"Damn!" The boys said in unison, as their eyes locked on Keisha's back side.

"Jazz, when you gonna stop faking and hit that?" Devin asked.

"Don't sweat mines D." Jazz smiled, then called Keisha over to the table. "Yo Keish!"

Keisha and all the girls in her crew looked good. All dimes with the exception of Trina, who could still get it.

Trina was cute in the face, but thick in the waist. She was a big girl, but she could dress. She stayed fresh and the confidence, swagger, and sex appeal made her the finest girl in the school, in Vincent's eyes.

Their other friend, Jessica, was a bad Spanish chick from South Omaha. She was built like a sister, flat stomach, and thin waist, with a nice round ass. Jessica was the quietest one in the group, and very laid back.

Their homegirl Gina, was a different story. She had a little waist with a fat ass. She's a beautiful ghetto fabulous redbone, with a snotty attitude.

All four girls were total opposites of each other but stuck together like glue. If you seen one of them, you would most likely see the others. If you got a problem with one of 'em, you would have a problem with all of 'em.

"What's up Keisha?"

"Nathen!" What's up with you Jazz? I see you found your crew today."

"Yeah, we in this motha fucka today," Vincent said.

"Glad to see y'all missed us," Chuck said, smiling because he knew some smart shit was coming.

"Ain't nobody miss y'all! We just glad y'all are here, because Jazz looked like he was about to cry yesterday without y'all," Gina said, as they all started laughing on their way to class.

∞ ∞ ∞ ∞ ∞ ∞ ∞ ∞ ∞

"Ok class quiet down. Quiet! Can I have your attention please?" The teacher yelled.

Ms. Dewaly was about what you would expect of a white woman teaching at a predominantly black and prejudice school. She had big breasts, a skinny frame, blue eyes, and pale skin that seemed to lack sunlight. She always smelled of stale coffee and too much perfume by J. Lo. She was twenty-seven years old and already losing her youthful glow.

"Can anyone tell me who or what they want to be when they get older?" …No hands! No volunteers! I guess I will have to choose someone myself," Ms. Dewaly said, scanning her class before choosing Devin. She really liked him, because he was the smartest and hardest working student in the classroom, a natural leader. He was never disruptive or disrespectful like most of the kids. Devin was also well liked by most of the students and teachers.

There was something about Devin. For his age, he was in control and stronger mentally than most students his age. Whenever Devin spoke, he did so in a smooth, but cocky manner. Whenever Ms. Dewaly would have a conversation with Devin, he would look deep into her blue eyes, making her feel some type of way between her legs; a way that she should not be feeling about her student. He had this sternness and such a caring soft touch she found so impressive, that sometimes it made her uncomfortable when she talked with him after class.

"Devin! Have you ever heard of Donald Trump or Warren Buffett?"

"Yeah, I've heard of 'em," said Devin. *Why she asking me about some white motha fuckas when ain't nobody white in this class, but her. Why not ask me about Bob Johnson or Oprah,* he thought to himself. He was annoyed, but decided against coming at his teacher so cold. "But they don't come up into many conversations in my neighborhood, it's more like Bob Johnson, Oprah, Magic Johnson, and Mike Jordan," said Devin.

"Oh, I see!" Ms. Dewaly said, not knowing why she was surprised by Devin's answers. "So, what do you see yourself being like? Or should I say what do you want to be when you get older?" She asked while noticing how Devin held the classroom's attention. He was really good at speaking in front of the class; comfortable, poised, and confident. It seemed as if he had wanted for her to call his name, as the other students were the exact opposite, praying that she didn't call their name at all.

"Well in my dreams I want to be a doctor, lawyer, dentist, or a pro athlete. But in real life, not dreaming, I look forward to being like people I see every day that got cheese; Mr. Goodwin, Mr. Dailey, or Big Jim," Devin said proudly.

"Devin who are those people?" Ms. Dewaly asked, with a puzzled look on her face.

"Well Mr. Dailey owns some stores, bars, and real estate around our way and Mr. Goodwin owns barber shops, stores, and real estate. Those are the successful role models that I have seen in my neighborhood," said Devin.

"Devin, you shouldn't give up on your dreams so easily."

"I'm not giving up! I still want to play pro basketball or football, but realistically I can see myself owning real estate and my own business a lot sooner," Devin said, with a look so serious that Ms. Dewaly was speechless, impressed, and turned on from his confidence.

Rrriinnggg! Rrring!

"Ok class we will continue this tomorrow," said Ms. Dewaly, after the bell sounded to change classes.

The hall in between classes was loud and packed as usual, with students trying to make quick conversations and shuffle along in the overcrowded halls to their next class, before the tardy bell rang.

"Yo! Where you headed?" Devin asked Chuck who was going in the opposite direction.

"Downstairs, my mom is suppose to pick me up and take me to Tray's funeral."

"That's what's up."

"I will be in the hood waiting on you after…"

"What's up Poppi?" Jessica interrupted, as she passed.

"What's poppin Mommi?" Devin answered with a big smile, watching Jessica's sexy walk, as she continued on down the hall.

"Damn! That bitch is so sexy." Chuck gave Devin a pound.

"Yeah, I got to quit bullshittin and turn up on that."

"Yeah, you've been fakin Poppi," Chuck said, laughing at his own comment.

"Them Vato Loco's be blocking homes," Devin said, pulling his pants up like one of the Mexican gang bangers.

"Fuck them! I wish I was the one she was throwing that pussy at. She would be in my bed saying ooh poppi, yes poppi."

"Boy you is brazy I'll holla at you later." Devin gave Chuck a pound, then walked into his next class.

Chapter 10

When Chuck and his mom entered Myers Funeral Home, the eulogy had just been given to the standing room only crowd. A line had formed to view Tray, who laid so peaceful in a marble red casket, at the front of the room. Only about five to ten people had a chance to shuffle past the casket and pay their respects, before gunfire erupted loudly outside the funeral home, sending those who were outside rushing inside, and sending a packed crowd of confused mourners who were inside, to dive on the floor, ducking behind walls. The shots seemed to last forever and when the deadly sound finally ended, the volley of shots had killed two and wounded three.

Chuck, who had grabbed his mom and took cover beneath a desk, looked out after the shots stopped. When everything seemed to be clear, he helped his mom up. She noticed Tray's mother, who was screaming and crying uncontrollably "Why! Why! Why!" And immediately ran over to console her. Not wanting to see his mom and his friend's mom in so much pain, Chuck went outside. People were everywhere crying, cussing, and getting into their cars. He saw a couple guys from the neighborhood with guns in their hands leaving, and knew that they were on their way to put in work. He wished he had a gun so he could ride out and put some work in too, but he didn't, plus he was with his mom. With a hostile feeling, Chuck went back into the disrespected funeral where he could see as he looked around, that everything was still in disorder.

"You ok?" Chuck asked, finally spotting his mom, who was talking to a lady he didn't know.

D. Christian

"I will call you later Ms. Loretha. I have to feed this boy before I take him home and head back to work."

"Ok Baby, you be careful and make sure you call me tonight, you hear!"

"I can't believe this shit! What is this world coming to? Crazy ass kids! They gonna drive that boy's momma to an early grave with this shit. What do you want to eat Boy? I want a fish sandwich from Lonnel's." Chuck's mom raged on and on without giving him a chance to answer, as she started the car and headed towards 16th Street to Lonnel's.

Chapter 11

The bus was finally coming around the corner after Chuck had been waiting for his friends for what seemed like hours to him. In real time it had only been thirty minutes since his mom had dropped him off at home, when he decided to walk to the bus stop in the middle of the projects to meet his friends.

"Man, y'all not gonna believe this shit. Them bitch ass niggahs came through and shot Trey's funeral up." Chuck blurted loudly and out of breath to his friends, as they made their exit off the bus and now stood around him on the sidewalk. "I think big Fred and Joe Willy from the Kellom side of the projects got shot up bad. They was standing outside in front of the funeral home when them niggahs came through blastin."

"Hell Nah!" Vincent exploded in anger. "Not another one of the homies from the hood." Vincent was furious that someone else he knew had lost their lives to this new thing called gang violence.

The pain and anger that Vincent felt, was felt by many, because living in the projects was like having one big family. When one family lost a family member, the loss was shared throughout the projects.

"Where dem niggahs from that did the blastin?" Asked Devin.

There were so many people at the funeral you couldn't see anything from inside after the shots rang out. People were all over the place running, ducking, hollering, and screaming. I heard that Tina that lives across the ballfield on the other side of the hood by 20th street, was outside in her car when the shooting started. I was gonna go holla at her, but I wanted to wait on y'all first."

"That's what's up let's go," said Vincent.

"While y'all go check that out, I'm gonna run home and get my heat."

"That's what's up D."

"Yo! I'm going with you D. we can take care of that business we talked about," Jamarl said.

"That's bool!" Devin said, as the crew split in opposite directions. Devin and Jamarl headed to Devin's house, while Vincent and Chuck walked across the ballfield to find the homegirl Tina.

"Damn, I should have told D to bring me back a sack." Chuck said, wanting to get to the money. "I need to buy me a strap!"

"Don't trip. I got a sack for you blood. Let's take care of this business first. Yo ain't that Tina?" Vincent pointed.

"Yeah, that's her. Yo T! T!" Chuck yelled, flagging Tina his way with his hands.

"What's brackin Chuck? That shit earlier was brazy hood. Soon as you and your mom went inside, I seen them niggahs creepin up like Menace to Society, hanging out the windows and shit like a movie dog, in slow motion. I wished I had my heat. I would have gotten off on them niggahs, but I was naked, so a bitch had to get low."

Vincent had no doubt in his mind about Tina getting at the niggahs if she had her gun. Tina was known to ride for the hood. Tina banged the hood set harder than some of the dudes in the hood.

"Did you see who was blastin?" Where dem niggahs from?" Vincent asked, his homegirl, who was probably the first female blood in Nebraska.

Her and a lot of Vincent's homies in the projects, were turned out in the early 80s by bloods from different sets in California, who migrated to the Midwest to make a bigger profit off their drug sales. Not only did they bring drugs, but they also brought their southern Californian gang culture with them; the crips and the bloods.

"Nah, dem fools had on flue rags that were covering their faces, probably 40th Ave or Hilltop. It don't matter though, they are both gonna get it Lil Homie," Tina said sternly.

"That's what I'm talking about. Holla at us we ready to ride for the hood and put that work in," Chuck said.

"On my hood. I was looking for y'all to holla at V anyways, to see how a bitch can cop some of that A-1 they say you got."

"Fo' sho we got that A-1. What's poppin?" Vincent said, feeling good about being wanted in the hood for something besides running errands.

"You know my trap house be jumpin on this side of the hood. I'm about to move into a house on 21st and Pratt though. So, if y'all want to rent my unit out from me, I'm down if you can get me a good price on that work."

"Homegirl, what cha trying to get?"

"I was gonna rent my spot out to Big Fred when I moved, but the homie is gone. So, if y'all give me the work for the low and pay the $300 a month for the section 8, the trap house is yours Little Homie. Y'all young niggahs ready or what?" Tina playfully challenged.

"No doubt! We ready," Vincent boasted. "What you trying to cop?"

"A couple juices if the price is right."

"Yo there goes Devin and Jamarl. Soo woo!" Chuck called to them, with the blood call. "Soo woo."

Devin and Jamarl ran up extremely active, greeting everyone with the signature blood handshake, locking fingers into a b.

"Sorry about what happened to your brother Jamarl. The homies put that work in last night for him, and we ain't done yet."

"That's what's up T, thanks," Jamarl said.

"So, what's up? Y'all want the spot or what? I already got most of my stuff moved out."

"Hold up! Let me holla at the homie," Vincent said, pulling Devin to the side. "Yo check this out D. T is trying to give us her trap spot for a good price on a couple ounces. All we gotta do is pay the bills because she's about to move. What you want to do? She got the best spot on this side," Vincent said, seriously.

Devin could not believe how shit was coming together so fast for him and his crew. Their own spot was exactly what they needed if they were gonna get to the real paper and that real paper is what Devin wanted. "No doubt! We gotta have it. T what you paying for an ounce from your people now?"

"Shit anywhere from a stack to twelve hundred. It depends Little Homie."

"I can do a stack everyday all day for you T. Give me about an hour and I'll be right back at cha. Yo V, we need to get a ride to go see old boy and dem."

"Y'all little niggahs don't know how to drive yet? Chuck, I know you can drive. Take my car. I need to finish packing my dishes and a few other things." Tina threw Chuck the keys to her car.

"That's what's up. Let's bounce Chuck," Devin said, already thinking of his next move. He was now playing chess, not checkers. The game had finally changed.

"Ima go with Tina to the spot so I can start pumping this A-1 out that bitch." Jamarl said proudly.

"If y'all wreck my shit, y'all paying for it," Tina said, as they walked off.

Chapter 12

It felt like the sun was shining on Devin as him and Chuck pulled up to the Spencer Projects. Devin's mind wheels were turning with thoughts of getting money. He no longer wanted to be like Mike. He wanted to be like Meech right now, as he scanned his surroundings.

Devin was barely out of the car when two fiends noticed him and approached trying to spend. "Let's go inside," Devin said, to the two customers and Chuck.

"Damn you already got it pumpin around here!" Chuck looked around, feeling out of bounds in the Spencers.

"Yo Bo! What's poppin? Where you at?" Devin yelled, as they walked right into his unit, since the door was open.

"I'm using the bathroom!" Bo yelled down the stairs.

"I was wondering what that smell was." Devin laughed, while serving the first two customers. As he was letting them out, two more came in.

"What took you so long D?" Bo asked, walking into the living room.

"I see it's poppin. This is my partner Chuck. Chuck this my niggah Bo. The Bo I was telling you about."

"Woop," Chuck greeted Bo, hands close to the big gun Devin gave him to hold. Chuck was very uncomfortable with all the nonstop traffic that had been coming in and out.

"Hey Chuck! Nice to meet you. D, I was wondering when you was gonna get here. Motha fuckas been coming around looking for you."

"I see this bitch is pumpin like Amoco."

"Here's the $80 I owe you and I was wondering if I could get a dub on two hundred dollars. I cashed my check already and I need to pay some bills," Bo lied. He really needed to make up for the money he had fucked off on some bad dope he bought and smoked up earlier. One hundred eighty-five dollars is all he had left to his name, from cashing his welfare check. "I'm trying to come up." Bo said, with high beamed big eyes.

I'm gonna look out for you Bo, but I ain't with that double up shit. I am trying to double up myself, but I got to take care of you for blessing me with this spot." Devin counted out like twenty pieces of crack and placed them in Bo's hands. "This is my rent, so don't come gaming with no lame shit, if you fuck it off smokin." Devin said sternly.

"What's up D? I was wondering if you made it," Lil Chris called through the screen door before walking in. "That bad bitch from last night just pulled up. She came through looking for you earlier too."

"Oh yeah!" Devin walked out onto the front porch, and waved for her to get out of the car and come in.

"Where you been all day cutie? I've been looking for you. Can you do me right?"

"No doubt I can do you right," Devin smiled, looking at the sexy young woman from head to toe. The pussy print on her jeans was so fat, and her flat stomach and small waist made her breasts look like delicious grapefruits, in her tight True Religion t-shirt. Devin refused to believe that this female could be a dope fiend, she was just too fine and freshly geared.

"You better be careful looking at me like that cutie," she smiled, noticing how Devin was all over her with his eyes.

"Excuse me, but I like money, and you look like a bag of money. You are beautiful Shawty," Devin smoothly flirted.

"Thank you," she said, slightly embarrassed by the way the young boy had her blushing. Can you dub me up again? You still got that A-1?"

"No doubt I got that good." Devin licked his lips like he was L. L. Cool J. He was feeling himself. "I can dub you up. What you trying to do?"

"Let me go to the car and see what my girl wants to do."

"Call her in," Devin said, wondering if she was fine like the girl standing in front of him.

"Ok hold up," she said, before going out to the front porch to tell her homegirl to come inside. When she came back inside, she was with a bad sexy looking tropical beauty. She looked like she was out of a Straight Stuntin Magazine. "Crisi, this is the young hustler I was telling you I got that A-1 from." She introduced Devin to the sexy dime piece.

"He's a cutie. How old are you?" She smiled.

"Age ain't nothing but a number. The last time I checked, it wasn't an age thing to getting money and my name is Devin. All of my friends call me D, not Little Cutie."

"It's nice to meet you D. My name is Crisi and my homegirl is Jackie, whom you already met."

"We didn't mean any disrespect. You are just the youngest hustler we done seen."

"No disrespect taken, cutie is just too soft to be called, in front of other niggahs," Devin smiled. "Let's handle business Crisi and Jackie."

"Let me get a dub on a hundred," Jackie said.

"Do you sell weight D?" Asked Crisi.

"What are you trying to get?"

"A half ounce later on when I cash my check, if the price is right."

"Five-hundred for you Beautiful," Devin winked his eye at Crisi, while he served Jackie her double up on a hundred dollars in twenty pieces.

"You got a number we can reach you at later?"

"Nah, I need to get me a cell phone."

"How long you gonna be here?"

"Ima be posted up for a while, as long as it keeps jumpin like this," Devin said, as Bo came through the door with money in his hands.

"Ok, we will be right back," Crisi said, before her and Jackie walked out the door.

"Damn! Them some bad bitches," Chuck said, staring out the screen door, looking at Jackie and Crisi's ass, while they walked to their car. "It's mutha fuckas everywhere out here now. I heard the Spencers had some bad bitches, but it's too much blue out here for me." Chuck said, backing away from the doorway.

Chapter 13

"Oh yeah D, I found out who them niggahs was that jacked you. I know two of them. They are from the projects over on Parker Street, by the cemetery. I caught up with that bitch Strawberry and beat her ass. She said it was Mike Mike and Little Ed, but she didn't know who the third dude was. Mike Mike and Little Ed usually hustle around here, but I haven't seen them around today," Bo explained.

"Yo Devin, old girl and them just pulled up," Little Chris yelled from the porch.

"Let me see that thang!" Devin grabbed the gun from Chuck before going outside. "Good looking out Chris." Devin dapped Chris, while he tucked the gun under his shirt with the other hand. Devin scanned his surroundings, as he walked towards the car; he was ready to pop off in broad daylight if and when he ever saw them niggahs that robbed him. "How y'all doing?" Devin spoke to a group of girls who looked about his age; sitting on the trunk of the car next to where Crisi had parked. He turned and gave them a quick look over, surprised they knew his name.

They all smiled and whispered something amongst themselves, as Devin got inside the Maxima. "What's up y'all?"

"Jackie got you a phone from her niggah at Verizon."

"Bitch! I don't got a niggah, especially that lame."

"Well anyways she got the lame to give her a phone for free."

"He thinks he's gonna get some of this wet wet." Jackie said, passing Devin the Verizon bag. "We already programmed it and put our numbers in. You probably got to put it on the charger when you go back inside, even though we had it charging with the car charger on the way back. Your phone number and other information about the phone is in the box."

"How much I owe for the hook up?" Devin asked, pulling out a fat stack of money.

"It's on me," Jackie said, staring at the stack of money Devin was holding.

"Well dinner is on me whenever," Devin said, placing everything in the bag, eyes locked on the blue Caprice that had turned onto Spencer Street from 30th.

"Damn! How old did you say you was?" Crisi asked, more impressed about how Devin carried himself. He had already proven to be smoother than a lot of niggahs her age.

"I didn't, I said age ain't nothing." *I know this ain't,* Devin thought while gritting and slouching down in the back seat, as the blue caprice pulled up and stopped in front of them.

"Got yo bitch ass!" Devin pulled the slide to make sure one was in the chamber.

"I told this ugly ass niggah I wasn't interested, and he keeps sweating a bitch," Crisi said venomously. "Ugh, I hope he don't get out and come over here."

Nah come on niggah, Devin said to himself, as he took his 45 automatic off safety.

"What niggah?" Crisi yelled, not knowing what was going on when she noticed the startled facial expression on Mike Mike's face. He went from showing his gold fronts smiling at Crisi and Jackie, to looking like a deer caught in headlights, as he took one step out the driver's side of the caprice.

BOK! Devin's first shot startled Jackie, Crisi, and everyone else that was close by, as it rang out loudly. Devin was halfway out of the backseat when Mike Mike noticed him. His mind was on revenge and murder when he got off the first shot.

Mike Mike scrambled to get back behind the steering wheel, as Devin's first shot exploded the driver's side window of the caprice, barely missing Mike Mike's head, giving him enough time to get out of park and into drive.

BOK! BOK! BOK! Devin was now all the way out of the back seat and on two feet, walking in the middle of The Spencers, dumping hot bullets into the back window and trunk of the fleeing Caprice.

"Yo bitch ass got lucky this time, but ima get at cha," Devin calmly said to himself, tucking his gun away and walking back to the Maxima like nothing ever happened. He opened the door and grabbed the Verizon bag. Jackie and Crisi sat frozen in the front seat, shaken up by what they had just seen. "Y'all get out of here before the police come. I'll call you later."

Devin closed the door and Jackie pulled off immediately.

"Come on Chuck let's bounce!" Devin yelled to Chuck, who was now on the porch.

"Why didn't you tell us you got jacked? I'm going to smoke them niggahs." Chuck climbed into the driver's seat of Tina's car and started the engine.

"That's just why I didn't say anything about it. We can't be out here on no reckless rah-rah shit like I just did. That was messy and careless. What if I had killed that niggah just now? I wouldn't be over here because it was all kinds of witnesses out there. The only good thing that can come from this miscalculated move, is that now everyone is going to know how we get down; for every action against us, it's gonna be a reaction. There's gonna be consequences and repercussions when you fuck with us."

"We don't need the heat, but this shit ain't over," Chuck responded.

"I gotta move differently and smarter. We gotta do better. We selling dope, so every move we make needs to be thought out and strategized carefully. That was two mistakes in two days, Chuck."

"I'm with whatever you're with my hitta, you put this shit together. Where we headed to now?" Asked Chuck.

"Take this left right here and go all the way to Spaulding Street," Devin said, dialing Black's number into his phone.

"Damn! What them bitches charge you for the phone?"

"It was a gift," Devin said, as someone answered on the other end of the phone.

Chapter 14

"Who this?"

"Lil D!"

"Who?"

"It's Lil Devin, Big Homie."

"Lil D in Omaha?"

"Yeah! What's up? We outside the house."

"We not there little homie, we back at the crib."

"Where at?"

"We in Cali Little Homie, not in Omaha. We won't be back until probably next week. I'm with Taco right now. We were just talking about you. Hold on." Black gave the phone to Taco.

"What's poppin Lil D, I heard you that niggah."

"I told you I was ready, but check this out Big Homie, I need to buy them shorts not the two pair of pants, because I can't fit them. I'll have the money in the bag for the shorts when you get back. I need the shorts Big Homie, it's hot out right now." Devin's mind was working in overdrive, as he did his best to get his point across to Taco without being messy and talking hot on the phone. He just hoped Taco picked up on the lingo.

Taco was confused at first, then it hit him all at once. The two and a half bricks he gave Devin to put up were the pants, and the half a brick was the shorts. "Blood this little niggah is sharp," Taco said to himself. "What happened to the clothes Black and JR gave you?"

"Tell 'em I said thanks. I wore them out already."

"You sure you don't want to wait until I get back? I'll be back in a couple days," Taco said, hesitant about giving the kid a whole half a brick, but if what Black and JR said about Devin's cooking game was true, he trusted Devin could handle it. So, he gave the ok, plus Taco really liked the young boy.

"No, I need to wear them now big homie. It's nice out here," Devin said.

Taco laughed and gave the ok. "Be careful Little Homie. I will call you later, I'm about to go in the mall. Is this the number I can reach you at?"

"Yeah, this is my new number. Big Homie do me another favor."

"What's that D?"

"Hook me up with some clothes and shoes. Cali got all the fly gear, that we don't have in Nebraska. I will pay you back when you get here," Devin said.

"I don't know what you like Lil D."

"Whateva you like Big Homie, you always got on some nice shit. That's how I'm gonna be; fresh every day," Devin responded.

"You working me like I'm your bitch, but I got you this time Little Homie. I'll get you right," Taco said.

"Good look, I will talk to you later," Devin said, hanging up the phone.

"What's up?" Asked Chuck.

"Ain't nobody here. They went back to Cali," Devin replied.

"What we gonna do now?"

"We gonna keep getting this money, that's what we gonna do, but first we need to go to the grocery store. I need some baking soda and one of those big Pyrex looking bowls, then you can drop me off at my house and I will meet y'all at the trap."

"What do you want me to tell Tina?"

"Tell her I am coming to take care of that, but we gonna need a stack for each one. We got that A-1. Oh yeah try to get us a scale."

"I know where I can get one," Chuck said.

Chapter 15

As soon as Devin entered the house, he made sure that his mom wasn't home before he grabbed the half a key of dope from his stash in the basement and left her a note on the refrigerator.

Mom I will be home around 10:00 tonight.

We have a basketball tournament in Elkorn.

My coach will bring me home.

Love you, Devin.

After placing the dope in his backpack and tucking the gun under his shirt, Devin headed to their new spot in the projects.

"What's up D? This spot is pumpin! I am almost done with that pack you gave me," Jamarl said, letting Devin in and the fiend he had just served out.

"Where is everybody?"

"Chuck went to the alley. Vincent and Tina went to pick up a scale. They all said they would be right back."

"Did Chuck have a grocery sack when he came in?"

"Yeah! It's on the kitchen table."

Devin sat at the kitchen table and took his time to untape the half a key he brought with him. He grabbed the Pyrex measuring bowl and baking soda out the sack, and poured a little of the baking soda and half of the dope into the bowl. The dope had a very strong odor. Devin added a little water to the bowl that was now on top of the stove. He turned the flame down and stirred the dope with a butter knife. He added a little more water as the dope became thick and pasty. He then whipped the dope.

"Yo Jamarl!"

"What's up D?" Jamarl said, coming into the kitchen.

"Don't' let nobody in the house. Serve 'em outside on the porch."

"Ok! Damn who taught you how to cook dope?" Jamarl asked, surprised to see Devin cooking dope.

"I learned by watching! It's not that hard," Devin said, adding more water to the thick paste of dope that was starting to gel.

"Damn! That shit is strong!" Jamarl said, covering his nose, as he watched Devin.

"Give me that bag of ice out of the freezer," Devin said, grabbing the bowl off the fire with a pair of potholders.

"Why you moving it around like that?" Jamarl asked.

"I'm about to make it all come back and lock up," Devin said, snapping his wrists and the bowl back and forth. The dope was sticking to the butterknife. He was just about ready for the ice when he heard the front door open. "Who is that Jamarl?" Devin grabbed his gun from underneath his shirt.

"It ain't nobody, but Vincent, Chuck, and Tina," Jamarl yelled back from the front room.

"Damn! What's that smell?" Vincent asked.

"Smell like dope!" Tina answered.

"Yo Chuck! Did you find a scale?" Devin asked from the kitchen.

"Yeah, I got one. We had to go to this little corner store called Cool Stuff, to buy a new one. It's a nice digital one," Chuck said, walking into the kitchen with the scale, and Tina right behind him.

"Wow! I didn't know y'all had it poppin like this!" Tina said, looking at all the dope in the kitchen.

"Do you have a big towel I can put this dope on?" Devin asked Tina.

"No! All my towels are already packed and gone, but I have a stack of old newspapers that you can use," Tina said, spreading the papers out on the table for Devin.

Devin dumped the large clumps of crack onto the newspaper.

"Where Jamarl go?" Devin asked.

"He's outside serving somebody. Why? What's up?" Vincent asked.

"We need a box of sandwich bags and some large Ziploc bags," Devin replied.

"I'll run to the store," Vincent said.

"Tina, do you want yours hard or soft?" Devin asked, before he cooked the rest of the dope.

Impressed, Tina said, "I'll take mine like that." She pointed to the hard-white clumps on the table.

"I gotcha!" Devin said, as he started cooking the rest of the dope.

Tina was very impressed, sitting in the kitchen watching Devin whip up the dope. She knew it had to be good, because of the smell and how fast it locked up.

"T you got any razors?" Devin asked.

"Yeah, look in that drawer by the stove," Tina said, looking out the window.

"Why you keep looking out the windows?" Devin asked, going into the drawer to get the razor to cut the dope.

"All that dope got me trippin, don't pay me no mind. Here goes your money and two sets of keys," Tina said, giving Devin the two thousand dollars and keys to the trap house.

Devin started counting the money after he placed the door keys in his pockets. He would give Vincent his key when he returned from the store.

"You said two stacks, right?" Tina asked, watching Devin count the money.

"Yeah! But if you keep spending with me, the prices will go down," Devin responded.

"What's your number. I already know I am gonna be calling you real soon! I know some people who are gonna want to get right," Tina said.

"That's what's up. You help me, and I'll help you get this money," Devin said, writing down his phone number on the newspaper for Tina.

"Damn! Where that fool at?" Devin asked, standing in the doorway getting some air and looking out the screen door for Vincent. He could see Jamarl at the end of the unit serving some fiend, but Vincent was not in sight. "Well, I guess I can still start weighing this shit," Devin said, walking back into the kitchen, with Tina right behind him.

"Devin you not scared of having all that dope?" Tina asked.

"A scared man can't make money," Devin said, pulling the gun from his waist, and placing it on the table next to him.

"I know that's right!" Tina said, looking at the gun and all the dope on the table. She had to give it to him, the boy was sharp to be so young.

When Vincent finally returned with the baggies and ziplocs, Devin had already weighed out twenty-four ounces and placed them in separate piles on the table, to be bagged up.

"Wow!" Vincent said, when he walked in the kitchen and saw all the dope on the table.

"Don't just stand there, help me bag this shit up. Each pile is an ounce," Devin said.

"Damn! We got twenty-four ounces out of that?" Vincent asked, counting the piles.

"Yeah, that shit comes back good and I didn't use that much soda," Devin said.

"Let's get it!" Vincent called out.

"Tina, here go your two ounces. Vincent, how many of these do you want now? I..."

"Knock Knock!" Chuck said through the screen of the locked front door. Startled, everybody in the kitchen froze for a second, until the voice registered.

"That ain't nobody, but Chuck," Devin said, as he placed his last ounce into the Ziploc.

"I'm gonna go let him in," Tina said, walking out of the kitchen, happy with her two ounces.

"Vincent, take these eight ounces for now and give me $6,000 dollars when you get it together. I want to pay Taco as soon as he gets back on Monday, and be able to buy some more dope," Devin said, putting the other fourteen ounces in his backpack.

"What's up?" Chuck said, coming into the kitchen.

"What's up with you, Homie?" Devin said, placing all the crumbs and pieces on the newspaper, into one large pile.

"This shit got 'em open, they're geekin for this A-1 we got. They passin them other hustlers up, looking for this bomb we got. I'm already out of dope," Chuck said.

"Me too!" Jamarl said, walking into the kitchen.

"Yo V, let me holler at you in the front room real quick," Devin requested.

"What's up D" Vincent asked, following Devin into the living room.

"I think this is what we should do, I'm gonna rock up the rest of them crumbs and pieces on the table and let Jamarl and Chuck keep it. When they are finished with that, you can put Chuck on, and I got Jamarl. Everybody else its $300 a quarter, $550 a half, and $1100 an ounce or you can sell it higher, its however you want to do it with yours. I'm just trying to keep this shit movin flip after flip, and we can still sell pieces out our traps," Devin replied.

"I don't care, I'm with whateva you're with. Let's get this money Homie," Vincent said, following Devin back into the kitchen.

"Here goes the money I owe you," Jamarl said, giving Devin the money when he came into the kitchen.

Devin placed the money in his pocket, then started rocking up the pile of crumbs and pieces that were on the table.

"When I get finished with this, you and Chuck can have it. Y'all don't have to pay for it this time," Devin said to Jamarl, as he watched all the crumbs and pieces gel together. Now all he had to do was let it cool. Devin used a little ice and cold water and the dope locked up into a nice big rock. Devin dumped the boulder onto the table. "Just weigh it and split it," Devin said to Jamarl and Chuck.

"Good looking out!" Chuck said, placing the boulder on the scale. "Eighteen grams." Chuck read the scale to Jamarl, then grabbed the razor and cut off nine grams for himself.

"Nine free grams!" I'm cool with that," Jamarl said smiling.

"Let me show y'all another flip!" Devin said, grabbing a razor. "Give me a gram Jamarl."

Jamarl weighed out a gram and gave it to Devin, who chopped the gram into seven small pieces. "Small pieces like this can sell for fifteen to twenty dollars a piece easily," Devin said. "It's on you how much love you gonna give and how much you want to make off your nine grams. That's just a little of the game I learned and I'm sharing it with y'all. If it was me, I would make $700 off a quarter, that's only seven grams Homie. You do the math," Devin said.

"I gotta bounce," Chuck said, bagging up his nine grams of crack, and placing it in his underwear.

"Where you headed to?" Vincent asked Chuck.

"I got this smokers car outside. I have to go pick her up from Sol's, a pawn shop not too far from the hood. I dropped her off to buy me a strap," Chuck answered.

"You got a fiend to get you a gun? You should have said something, we could have gotten a couple of 'em. I need one too," Vincent said.

"She said she got the hook up. Don't trip," Chuck replied.

"I will sell you my glock, with two extra clips for a half ounce," Tina said to Vincent.

"That's what's up. I need that ASAP Homegirl," Vincent said.

"Hey V! Have me something ready later! I'll call you when I am finished with these nine grams," Chuck said, going out the door.

"Tina when can I get that strap?" I got that half you want right here," Vincent asked.

"It's at the other house. Help me take the rest of these boxes to the car, then we can go get it." Tina said, picking up a box, heading out the door.

"Yo T! Let me get a ride home. I only stay a few..."

"I know where you live, you better hurry up," Tina replied, cutting Devin off.

"Hey Jamarl, hold the trap down. I will be right back," Devin said, grabbing his backpack off the kitchen table.

Devin ran and jumped in the back seat of Tina's car. He didn't like having all the dope on him, and couldn't wait to get home to put it up.

As Tina was pulling away from the curb, Vincent noticed Champaine trying to flag them down.

"Pull over Tina! Let me make this sell real quick. She always spends at least a hundred dollars," Vincent said.

"Fool we dirty! Tina don't pull this car over," Devin said sternly.

Tina was about to pull over for Champaine until Devin said something. Tina was familiar with the parttime hooker, fulltime fiend, but didn't stop like Vincent requested. She listened to Devin and kept going.

"V, we got a half a bird hard in this car, and you think we gonna pull over for a hundred-dollar sale to a fiend on a hot block? Come on with that dumb shit, Vincent. All money ain't good money, our game gotta be tighter than that. That's slippin Homie," Devin said.

"I'm not pulling over anyway. Damn! There go the po-pos up there at the stop sign. Take off y'alls caps," Tina said.

Devin and Vincent quickly snatched off their caps, fastened their seat belts, and looked straight ahead, as they passed by the police car. It was like everyone in the car was holding their breath until the car was out of sight.

"Shit! That was close, and you wanted to pull over for a sale on this hot ass street, with the police coming around the corner and everything. That's all we need is to get caught up, because they thought we was trying to buy some pussy from that crackhead hooker," Devin said.

"That's my bad, I wasn't thinking. I forgot we had all this dope in the car," Vincent said.

"We always gotta be on our toes thinking now V. We in the game and this shit is real Homie. Don't pull up in the front of my house, let me out in the back," Devin said.

"What cha about to do?" Vincent asked Devin.

"Put this dope up, then go back to the trap with Jamarl. I'll probably go to the Spencers later around 6:00 pm.

"That's what's up Homie. I'll be back through, after I get this strap," Vincent said.

"I'll be calling you later," Tina said, pulling over to the curb to let Devin out.

"Holla at y'all later!" Devin said, closing the back door of the car.

"Devin ran from the back of the alley to the front of his house. When he saw his mother's boyfriend's car, he knew that she was home.

"Hi Mom!" Devin spoke to his mom, who was sitting in the front room watching Oprah on TV, when he came in the front door.

"I thought you had a game?" Devin's mom asked.

"I'm on my way, I forgot my basketball shoes," Devin replied, going up to his room. When Devin got to his room, he locked the door behind himself, took the dope out of the backpack, and grabbed an ounce out of the Ziploc before stashing the dope in one of the speakers. *I don't need all this money on me,* Devin thought to himself, opening the other speaker then counting $2,000 dollars out of his pockets, and placing it in his stash with the rest of his money. Devin turned and looked inside his room to make sure everything was in place, before he headed downstairs with his backpack.

"Mom where is your friend? Ain't that his car outside?" Devin asked, walking into the front room.

"Yes! That's his car I have to pick him up from work later. I might not be here when you get home, so make sure you got your key before you leave. Did you eat yet?" Devin's mom asked.

"The coach is gonna get us pizza after the game," Devin answered.

"Good luck!" Devin's mom said.

"See you later! Love you," Devin said, going out the door. Devin paused on the porch to make sure his mom wasn't coming out the door or looking out any of the windows, before he headed around to the back of the house to get his bike, so he could go back to the trap house.

Chapter 16

"That's what that sound was," Devin said to himself, getting off his bike in front of the project unit. The techno music coming from his pocket was the strange noise he was hearing on his way to the projects. Devin reached into his pocket and pulled out his phone that had two missed calls. I gotta change my ringtone, this techno shit is bammer,"

"Yo Jamarl," Devin called out into the furnitureless house.

"I'm up here taking a shit," Jamarl yelled down the stairs.

Devin's phone started playing the techno music again. "I have to hurry up and get this shit off of here," Devin said, answering the phone. "Hello!"

"Why do you have a phone if you are not going to answer it?" Bo asked.

"They got this crazy ringtone on it. I didn't even know that it was ringing. What's up Bo?" Devin asked.

"When are you coming through? You're missing a lot of paper," Bo said.

"I'll be there in a minute. I need to take care of something first.

"Hurry up. I'll see you when you get here," Bo said, hanging up.

Devin hung up the phone, and immediately changed his ringtone.

"What's up D? It's been rolling ever since y'all left. I only have three grams left," Jamarl said, giving Devin a pound.

Knock! Knock! Knock!

"I got it," Jamarl said, going to the door.

"What's up Shawn?" Jamarl said, letting one of the homies in.

"I heard y'all got that butter," Shawn said.

Devin remembered Shawn from hoopin at Kellom, but he hadn't seen him in a while. The last Devin heard, Shawn was sent to Kearney, the youth authority in Nebraska, to be locked up. "When you get home?" Devin asked.

"Last week, I just been laying low, trying to keep happy. What's up with you D? you still hoopin?" Shawn asked.

"Yeah, I still get it in," Devin replied.

"Where Vincent at? I heard y'all got the best dope around here right now."

"He should be back in a minute. Why what's up?" Asked Devin.

"My people got some bullshit dope right now. I was looking for Vincent to try and buy a quarter if he was holdin like that."

"How much you got?" Devin asked.

"$350 that's what they go for," Shawn stated, in a sarcastic tone.

"Uh-Uh! That's what they use to go for. Give me $300 and I got you Homie," Devin said.

"Word!" Shawn exclaimed, surprised.

"Hold up," Devin said, going into the kitchen to weigh out a couple quarters from the ounce he had brought with him.

"Damn! I only been gone a couple months and y'all already in the game. When I left, Devin was still going to the Boys Club every day and your brother wouldn't let you off the porch."

"We off the porch now and my brother is gone," Jamarl stated, in an agitated tone.

"My bad Little Homie, and I didn't mean to bring that up. I got love for your brother, he was my O.G. I'm ridin for him."

"Don't trip. I'm gonna put that work in too," Jamarl said.

"That was then, and this is now. I still go to the Boys Club, but we gettin that money every day, and we ridin for the hood. Don't get that twisted," Devin said, coming back into the room with Shawn's quarter ounce in his hand.

"This that bomb Chuck and Vincent got?" Shawn asked, before he gave Devin the $300.

"No doubt!" Devin said, giving Shawn the quarter.

"Good looking out Homie," Shawn said, giving Devin the $300, before he left.

As soon as Shawn walked out, there was a knock on the door. Jamarl opened the door and Devin watched to see who it was.

"What's up Suzzie? What cha tryin to get?" Jamarl asked.

"Let me get $30," Suzzie requested.

"Here you go," Jamarl replied, servin Suzzie the crack.

"Y'all got someone else out here," Suzzie said, pausing before she went out the door, letting the other fiend in.

"What do y'all 50's look like?" The man asked, pulling his money out.

"We got the boulders. This ain't the alley big man and it's bomb dope," Devin said, breaking off a piece, then showing it to the man.

"Uh-huh," the man said, giving Devin the $50 dollar bill.

"Let 'em know this where the bomb is at," Devin said, letting the man out.

"This where y'all gonna be at? I'll be back," the man said, looking at the size of his rock one more time before he left.

"D, I'm gonna bounce to the house real quick. I haven't been home yet, and its 5:40 pm. You gonna be here when I get back?" Jamarl asked.

"I don't know. Here, take this quarter ounce just in case I'm gone when you get back."

"How much do I owe you?"

"$250," Devin said.

"I have that now here you go," Jamarl said, counting the money he took out of his pockets to give to Devin. "$250. Here come a couple swerves." Jamarl went out the door.

"You holdin?" The swerve asked Jamarl, who turned around and pointed at Devin standing in the doorway.

Devin opened the screen door and let the two swerves in.

"What y'all tryin to get?" Devin asked.

"I want a 20 piece."

"Let me get one for $45," the other man said.

Devin served both men before letting them out and closing and locking the screen door behind them. We gotta hurry up and get some furniture, Devin thought, noticing he had nowhere to sit in the front room. He went into the kitchen to grab a chair to sit on. He was headed back to the front room with the chair, when he heard someone trying to come into the back door.

"Who Dat?" Devin asked, going to the back door with his gun out and ready.

"Who you think it is?" Vincent asked, opening the door. "Me and you are the only ones with keys, right?"

"Yeah, for now, but we gotta get some made for Jamarl and Chuck. Why did you come in through the back?" Devin asked.

"Because you can't see the backdoor from the street like you can the front. The front door is in the open and you can see everything. I saw the fiend you just served leaving out when we were pulling up. So, from here on out, we gonna have all the traffic come to the back door. No more servin from the front door. We gonna serve in the kitchen only. That way when we have company, they can't be all in our business."

"Alright I like that," Devin said.

"Rrring! Rrring!"

"Hello!" Devin answered his phone.

"What's up Baby? Where you at?" The sexy voice asked.

"I'm in the projects what's up wit cha Jackie?"

"That's that bad bitch from the other day?" Vincent asked, his voice urgent, as he listened in on Devin's conversation.

"Yo! Yooo!" A voice called through the front screen.

"Go get the door wit your nosey ass!" Devin said to Vincent, covering the phone with his palm.

"How'd you know it was me?" Jackie said.

"How can I forget a sexy voice like yours?"

"Boy, you're gonna make me put it on you."

"If you're not careful, I'm gonna end up putting it on you," Devin laughed in astonishment.

"What's up though? I know you didn't call me to talk dirty on the phone. Hold on for a sec," Devin said, hearing a knock at the kitchen door.

"I got it," Vincent said, coming into the kitchen. "I had them go around to the back."

"So, where you at Jackie?" Devin asked, getting back on the phone.

"In front of your spot about to come in."

"I'm not at that spot, I'm at my other spot."

"Where is that?"

"Do you know where the Logan Fontenelle Projects are?"

"Yeah, down on 24th Street," Jackie responded

"That's right, but I am on the 20th Street side of the hood."

"I'm on my way."

"Ok, call me when you get to the phone booth on the 20th Street side," Devin said, hanging up his phone.

"We need some furniture!" Vincent exclaimed, walking into the empty front room.

"I was just thinking that myself. Have you been upstairs yet?" Devin asked on his way up the stairs.

"No," Vincent said, following Devin up the steps. They looked in the bathroom first and then the two bedrooms.

"Which bedroom do you want?" Vincent asked.

"This one is cool," Devin said, looking at the view outside the bedroom window. He could see the phone booth on 20th and when he looked to the left, he could see across the ballfield.

"We need to get some beds and TVs. We can have our spot laid like Taco's. We just gotta find somebody to get what we need," Vincent stated, in an undecided tone.

Rrring! Rrring!

"Hello!" Devin answered.

"I'm at the phone booth, Boo."

Devin looked out the window and saw Jackie's clean Maxima. "I'm on my way out," Devin said, hanging up the phone.

"Where you headed? Home?" Vincent asked, following Devin down the steps.

"I'm about to go to the Spencers."

"Alright be careful Homie."

"I got my heat," Devin said, in a serious tone.

"Oh yeah, I didn't even show you my glock," Vincent said, pulling his gun from his belt.

"I like that!" Devin said, grabbing his backpack off the table. "Yo! Jamarl said he would be back in a minute and I haven't seen Chuck yet," Devin said, headed out the front door.

"Don't trip! I'll hold it down," Vincent said, watching his friend walk to the clean Maxima. "Oh yeah hey D!"

"What's up?" Devin turned around.

"Ask Jackie what she will charge to get me a phone?" Vincent yelled.

"Will do Homie," Devin turned back around and got in the car.

Chapter 17

"What's up Boo?" Jackie asked, when Devin got in the car and closed the door.

"What's up wit cha sexy? Damn! You look good," Devin said, licking his lips and biting down on his bottom lip, looking at Jackie from head to toe.

Jackie had on a form fitting summer dress and some Coach sandals. When she turned to put the car in drive, her dress rode up her thighs, showing more of her sexy chocolate legs. Even Jackie's feet looked good to Devin. She had a fresh pedicure, toes painted red, decorated in diamonds and glitter. Jackie could see Devin checking her out from head to toe, biting down on his bottom lip, and it was turning her on.

"So, what's up Beautiful? What are you trying to get?" Devin broke out of the spell Jackie's body and perfume was putting on him.

"I got $150 and Crisi wants to spend $100. I have to pick her up from work later."

"Here take this," Devin said, passing Jackie a quarter ounce.

Jackie's eyes got big looking at all that dope in her hand. "I only got $150," Jackie said, trying to pass the dope back to Devin.

"I thought you said Crisi has $100 on it?"

"I did, but she don't get off work until 8:00pm."

"Just bring me my money when she gets off," Devin said, sternly.

Rrring! Rrring! Rrring!

"Turn that music down a little please," Devin said, answering his phone. "Hello."

"What's up D? This is Tina."

"What's up homegirl?"

"I need two of 'em like before," Tina requested.

"Where you at?" Devin asked.

"Club 2000. I'm with my homeboy."

"I need two stacks, and I'm not trying to meet nobody new."

"That's cool! Where you at?"

"Hold on! I'm in traffic," Devin replied to Tina, then asked Jackie a question. "Do you know where Club 2000 is?"

"Yeah," Jackie replied. "It's not far from here."

"Hello Tina!"

"Yeah, what's up?"

"I'll call you when I am outside. I'm coming to you," Devin said, erasing the screen on the phone

"Devin do you need me to take you to Club 2000?" Jackie asked.

"Yeah, but take a right up here on Lake Street, then another right when you get to 20th." *I hope my mom is gone*, Devin thought to himself, as he looked down 20th Street to see if he could see his mom's boyfriend's car. "Awww yes," Devin smiled weakly, thankful he did not see the car.

"Stop at that big white house," Devin pointed.

"Right here," Jackie said, pulling up to the curb in front of Devin's house.

"Yeah, I'll be right back," Devin said, getting out the car.

Devin ran up to the door, unlocked it, and then ran up to his room two steps at a time. Devin wasted no time opening his speaker with the Ziploc of dope in it, taking out three ounces. When he was finished, he put the stash back in the speaker and one ounce of dope in his pocket. Then he went to the kitchen to get a small paper sack for the two ounces, before he ran back to the car.

When Devin got back in the car, Jackie had "Plies, The Real Testament" bumpin through the speakers. "It was my fault fool I keep it too real," Devin vibed along with the music, as Jackie headed to Club 2000.

"Woulda did ah hundred years for ya, because I fuck wit ya/you taught me what a good heart in these streets a get ya/not ah mu'fuckin thang, but a sad picture," Devin sang along to the music once again. He was stuck on Jackie's sexy body. Her summer dress had risen up further than before, and Devin couldn't take his eyes of her legs.

Jackie noticed Devin checking her out again from the corner of her eye, so she gave him something to look at, spreading her legs wide enough so that her dress rode all the way up, exposing her freshly shaved pussy.

Damn, Devin said to himself.

Jackie could read his lips and see him biting down on his bottom lip again. *Damn! This boy got me on fire.* She noticed the nice size bulge in his pants. *I wonder if he is working with all that*, Jackie thought to herself. "We are almost there," Jackie said out loud, breaking out of the trance the young boy put her in.

"Damn Baby," Devin said, eyes locked on Jackie's pussy, while he took out his phone and called Tina back at the number she called from.

Rrring! Rrring!

"Hello!" A male voice answered.

"Tell Tina I am outside."

"Ok!" The man said hanging up.

When Devin saw Tina come out the club, he reached over and hit the horn, motioning her over to the car with a wave. When she crossed the street, Devin motioned for her to get in the back seat.

"Drive around the block," Devin told Jackie, when Tina got in the car. "What's up Homegirl?" Devin said to Tina, turning around in his seat.

"Trying to get this money," Tina said, passing Devin the $2,000 dollars and at the same time trying to figure out who this chick was that was driving. *She looks too young to be his mom, but too old to be his girl and they didn't look like sister and brother,* Tina thought.

"Here you go," Devin said, giving Tina the two ounces, after he counted the money.

"I'll holla at cha later D," Tina said, about to get out, as they pulled back up in front of Club 2000.

"Alright Homegirl," Devin said, as Tina got out the car.

"Damn! I didn't know you had it like that," Jackie said, pulling off.

"It's a lot that you don't know about me, but it's a lot that I want to show you about me."

"This is crazy, but I want you to show me," Jackie said, confused about what she was feeling.

"Jackie, I need you to do something for me!"

"What's that Boo?"

"I need another cell phone and some furniture for my spot."

"Your spot?" Jackie asked confused.

"Yeah, I got my own spot, but its empty right now. I need everything. Can you help me? I got the money, don't trip."

"I think I can handle all that. Plus, Crisi has the hook up on credit cards. You gonna let me be your home decorator when she gets some fresh credit cards?"

"I don't care. I just want to be comfortable," Devin said.

"I gotcha Boo. Do you want to go get the phone now?" Jackie asked.

"No. I got something to handle. You can drop me off in the Spencers first and go take care of that by yourself, while I check on this money, then come back and get me," Devin said.

"Ok," Jackie said, heading to the Spencer Projects.

Bo's house was already packed when Devin got dropped off. Devin made eight quick sales before the house was cleared.

"Damn!" Devin said, feeling the wads of cash he had stuffed into his front pocket.

"It's always like this the first of the month," Bo said. "You have something for me for this $80," Bo said, giving Devin the money.

"Take this," Devin said, breaking Bo off some nice pieces. "Bo you better have some money to get back on. Don't fuck this off."

"Oh yeah! I forgot to tell you Lil Chris been looking for you," Bo said, looking at the rocks Devin gave him.

"Is he next door?"

"I think so. He just left from over here about twenty minutes ago"

The sun was setting, but the projects were alive and poppin. Devin went next door to see if Lil Chris was home. He knocked on the door and kept his eyes on his surroundings, suspicious of everything moving in the projects.

"What's up D?" Lil Chris asked, opening the door to let Devin in.

"What's up with you?" Devin walked in, closing the door behind himself.

"Where you been at? It's been rolling around here. Me and a couple of my friends are trying to get some double ups."

"You trying to get some work?" Devin asked, surprised.

Yeah, I need a dub on $50. I might as well get this money. I already know what to do from watching my dad and being out here all the time. I could be getting all the money that you are missing when you're not here. I gotta be here Homie. I live here. Come on Homie. I know what I am doing. I can help you and you can help me. I'm either gonna get it from you or somebody else. I'm gonna get it though, because I'm tired of being broke." Lil Chris said.

"I hear you and I feel what you are saying, but this shit is real, this ain't a movie Lil Chris. You see what happened to me?" Devin said.

"This is my hood right here. The people around here know me. I respect you for coming back and being about your business. You got the trap pumping, but I'm here all the time. I can make it boom!" Lil Chris stated, in a serious tone.

"Ok! This is what I'm gonna do, I am gonna front you a half ounce for $600 and see how long it takes for you to get it off."

"Shit, it's the first of the month. It won't take me long," Lil Chris said, happily.

"I hear you!" Devin said, giving Lil Chris the half ounce.

Knock! Knock!

"Who is it?" Lil Chris yelled, opening the door.

"Devin in there?" Bo asked.

"Yeah, hold up here he comes," Lil Chris said, moving outside to let Devin out.

Rrring! Rrring!

"Hello." Devin answered his phone and headed out the door.

"I'm pulling up Boo, you ready?" Jackie asked.

"Yeah! I see you, here I come," Devin said, hanging up his phone. "Yo Lil Chris, I'm about to bounce. Take care of that business over Bo's for me." Devin headed out the door.

"What's up young D?" Pimpin Slim said to Devin, on his way into Bo's.

"What's up Pimpin? I gotta bounce, but you can holla at my homeboy," Devin said, pointing to Lil Chris.

"I see you young D. Keep pimpin," Slim said to Devin, as he ran to the Maxima, with the beautiful chocolate dime piece behind the wheel.

"24-7 Slim," Devin said, getting into the car.

"What's up Boo? You got somewhere else you need me to take you, or do you want to ride with me to pick up Crisi?"

"It don't matter I'm good either way. Whateva is best for you."

"Well, I am keepin your sexy chocolate ass with me," Jackie said.

"Ok that's cool, but you are the one that's sexy chocolate," Devin said relaxing back into the seat, enjoying the ride.

"The phone is in the back seat. I didn't charge it up, but it's already programmed," Jackie said.

"How much I owe you?"

"Nothing! I got this thing going with this lame that works there. He hooks me up for free thinking he's gonna get some of this! Just pay the bills on time and I got you, whateva you need," Jackie said.

"Thank you!" Devin said, pulling out the large wad of cash he had stuffed in his pockets at Bo's."

"Damn!" Jackie said, impressed with all the money Devin had in his lap.

After counting his money, Devin relaxed back in the seat and closed his eyes, thinking about Crisi and Jackie. They were so beautiful and smart. Why were they smoking this crack shit? After riding in silence for the last ten minutes, debating on if he would ask Jackie about smoking crack or not, Devin broke the silence.

"Jackie, why y'all smoke this crack shit?"

"Fool! You got the game fucked up; we don't smoke this shit. D I've been hustlin since I was fourteen. Ever since my dad left, I've been boostin clothes, credit cards, vouchers, and all kinds of scams. My momma turned me out. We would clean tricks and stores out. She had me doing all kinds of things when I was younger. Yeah, it sounds fucked up, but I have never wanted for nothin, I have always been spoiled with the best. When my dad left, my mom laced me to the game early. As for this crack shit, this is a new hustle. Me and Crisi noticed all the money to be made. We both have family members and friends who spend lots of money on this shit all the time, so we decided since they wanted it, we would have it. They aren't the type to go to the projects, and most of the whites in their neighborhoods mess with powder, not crack. Plus, they hook us up with the fake ID's, credit cards, and checks. Our people got that money, and all the frauds to get paper, but love this crack." Jackie explained.

"What's up wit Crisi?" Devin asked.

"That's my girl! Crisi moved in with me and my mom when we was in the eighth grade together. Her stepdad was touching and beating on her. Crisi's mom didn't believe her when she told her about his sexual abuse, so my mom convinced her mom to let Crisi move with us. She is cool, a real go getter. All she wants to do is smoke weed and spend money, like me." Jackie said.

"Y'alls boyfriends must have some deep pockets, because you two stay fly, and this Maxima is nice."

"D, you got us twisted. We don't need no boyfriends to shine. We got each other. We make our own cake. Everything we got, we got with our own money. Nobody gave us shit," Jackie said, pulling into the parking lot of Crisi's job.

Devin opened the front door to get in the back when he noticed Crisi coming out of the building. He couldn't help but admire her beauty. 36-29-40 and Dominican with a Dominican and black mother and a white father. Her mocha complexion and pretty eyes glowed in the dark. "She's thick in all the right places," Devin said to himself, checking Crisi out, as she got in the front seat.

"What's up D? You didn't have to get in the back," Crisi said.

"I'm cool. I like looking at both of y'all anyway," Devin smiled and closed the door.

"What's up Babe?" Crisi said to Jackie.

"Nothing, been running around all day."

"Here! Devin gave us this for $250. I already gave him $150," Jackie said, throwing the quarter ounce onto Crisi's lap.

"Thanks D," Crisi said, handing Devin a $100 bill out of her Michael Kors purse.

"It ain't nothing," Devin said, placing the $100 bill on top of his roll of money.

"Y'all hungry? Because I am!" Exclaimed Jackie.

"I've had a taste for Red Lobster all day," Crisi said.

"That sounds good to me too," Jackie responded.

"I'm starving! How far is that from here?" Devin asked.

"It's not that far."

"Well Red Lobster it is," Devin said, as he relaxed in the backseat, enjoying the new scenery out the window. All Devin knew was that he was out west, and far from home.

Chapter 18

The parking lot at Red Lobster was full. Jackie had to drive through it for about five minutes, before they found a parking spot. The lobby was the same, standing room only. Devin, Crisi, and Jackie waited to be seated at a table, while Jacki and Crisi chatted about shopping, and Devin stared at the large saltwater aquarium. Devin was focused on the colorful fish, until he saw Jessica out the corner of his eye with three guys and a woman, probably her mom, dad, and two brothers. They looked like a rich Mexican family. Her dad had on jeans with a nice button up shirt, a snakeskin belt that matched his boots, and a large fancy belt buckle. Jessica and her mom both had on nice dresses. You could see where Jessica got her looks from, because her mom was beautiful.

The two younger men looked like gang bangers in their Dickies pants and Oakland Raider's jackets. Devin was hesitant to speak because of her family, and was gonna just let the sexy Jessica and her family walk out the door, until Jessica caught him gawking and smiled.

"Dispense usted!" (Excuse me!) Devin said in Spanish.

"Como esta usted Poppi?" (How are you?)

"Muy bien gracias," (Very well thanks.) said Devin.

"Usted Espanol?" (You speak Spanish?) Jessica questioned in a surprised tone.

"Un poco," (A little.) Devin replied, as Jessica's family waited. It wasn't long before her two brothers got curious and came over. They had never seen their sister talk to any other males besides family, and on top of that, this guy was black, and their sister seemed to be elated to see him.

"You got company coming and they don't look happy," Devin whispered, keeping his eyes on the two brothers.

"Muy buenas noche." (A very good night to you!) Jessica said, in a serious tone, turning around to leave.

"Hasta manana." (See you tomorrow.) Devin said smiling.

"She's so cute, what's her name?" Crisi asked.

"Who her? Oh, that's Jessica, we go to the same school," Devin said, in a shaken voice.

"You hit that yet?" Jackie asked, with admiration.

"Nah, not yet!" Devin said, caught off guard by Jackie's forwardness.

"You know she likes you right?" Jackie asked.

Devin just shrugged it off as nothing.

"Your table is ready. Please follow me," the waitress said, turning to lead them to their table. They were seated in a cozy booth, Devin on one side, and Jackie and Crisi on the other.

"I will be your waitress," the young voluptuous blond said, placing the menus on the table. "Would you like to order any cocktails, before I bring out your bread?"

"Yes, let us have two vodka and cranberry drinks on ice. What you drinking Devin?" Jackie asked, before passing her and Crisi's fake IDs to the waitress.

"I'll take a large coke," Devin replied, looking at his menu, trying to decide between shrimp and lobster. It had been a while since Devin went to a seafood restaurant. He remembered the summers he would go out of town to stay with his grandmother, and she would always fry shrimp, grill steak, and cook crab legs. Just the thought of seafood made him think about his grandmother.

"Here are your drinks. Are you ready to order, or should I come back?" The waitress asked.

"Do y'all know what you want?" Devin asked, closing his menu, with his mind made up on what he wanted.

"Yes! Let me get the shrimp feta cheese pasta," Jackie ordered.

"I'll take the half pound of crab legs special, with mashed potatoes," said Crisi.

"And for you Sir?"

"Let me get a half pound of crab legs and the fried shrimp and lobster dinner," Devin replied.

"I'll be back with your orders shortly," the waitress said, turning toward the kitchen.

"You gonna eat all that?" Jackie asked Devin.

"No doubt! I love seafood," Devin responded, just as the waitress came back around with a nice hot batch of biscuits.

"That's funny, because me and Crisi are the same, we come here a lot," Jackie said. "Try the bread Poppi!" Jackie smiled jokingly at Devin about earlier, hearing Jessica call him Poppi.

"They got the best biscuits," Crisi said, buttering the bread then passing it to Devin.

"Mmmm, this is good," Devin said, taking another bite of his biscuit. "Crisi let me taste your drink," Devin asked, reaching for her glass of vodka and cranberry.

"Here, you go ahead and sip on this, just don't let the waitresses see you. I'm gonna order another one," Crisi said, sliding the glass across the table to Devin.

No one noticed because of the good food, drinks, and good conversation, that they had been in the restaurant for over two and a half hours.

"We better get ready to leave, if you still want to go to Hanks tonight Jackie," Crisi said, motioning for the waitress to bring their check.

"Yeah, I still want to go, on Thursdays Hanks has the biggest crowd. We gotta get Devin a fake ID when we talk to Pam."

"We have to make it soon because your birthday party is coming up, and you know Club 1507 downtown is gonna card," Crisi said.

"Hanks? 1507? You talkin about clubs?" Devin asked. "I'm not thinking about no club. Drop me off at my spot, money is the only club I'm trying to get into," Devin said, reaching for the bill the waitress placed on the table.

"How much is it?" Jackie asked, reaching into her purse.

"Don't trip," Devin replied, placing $130 in the folder before getting up.

The ride home from the restaurant was unsteady and long for Devin. The alcohol was getting the best of him. He rode with his head pressed to the window, trying to get more air while Crisi and Jackie talked about what they would wear to the club. Just hearing what the two beautiful women planned on wearing, had Devin thinking about changing his mind about going to the club.

Chapter 19

Rrring! Rrring! Rrring!

"Hello!" Devin answered.

"What's up D? I got that for you. It's been going down since you left. You gonna come through tonight and pick it up or do you want me to hold on to it until tomorrow? I'm not out or nothing like that I am still holdin," Lil Chris said, pausing for Devin's answers.

"Damn, you done already. I'll be through there in a minute," Devin said, closing up the phone. Yo! Jackie take me to the Spencers first, before you drop me off. Do you got enough time?" Devin asked, trying to pull himself together and get focused.

"I gotcha Boo just make it quick," Jackie said, making a right on 30th and Ames.

"It won't take long. I just need to pick up something," Devin said, pressing the phone's send button from his last incoming call. He listened, as the phone that Lil Chris had just called from rang several times.

"Hello!"

"Check this out Lil Chris, I'm about to pull up in the front, come out to the car."

"Ok!" Lil Chris said, hanging up the phone.

"Boy! You are not gonna be running in and out of my house! You need to sit yo ass down somewhere." Lil Chris's mom said to his back, as he shut the door behind himself on the way out to meet Devin, who just pulled up in the parking lot.

Chris could not believe Devin was still with the women in the Maxima. He noticed Devin in the backseat, motioning for him to come over.

"What's up Lil Chris?" Devin said, giving him a pound when he got in the backseat.

"The first of the month, that's what's up; getting this money," Lil Chris said, pulling a large rubber banded roll of money out of his pocket, and handing it to Devin. "It's all there."

"That's what's up. I'll bring an onion over here tomorrow for you when I get out of school, unless you need it tonight?"

"Nah, I'm cool. I still got about a quarter left."

"Damn! I see you on the grind for real Lil Chris, that's what's up," Devin said, admiring Lil Chris's hustle.

"I can't let you be the only young hustler out here gettin money. I'll holla at you tomorrow," Lil Chris said, getting out of the car, spotting some fiends that had been spending money with him all day.

"See you tomorrow Homie," Devin said, unrolling the banded money. "Thanks Jackie! You can drop me off in the hood where you picked me up at," Devin said, counting his money.

"Devin what school you go to?" Jackie asked, pulling out of the Spencers.

"Norris! Why? You gonna pick me up after school tomorrow?" Devin asked.

"Norris? I know you lying boy!" Jackie exclaimed, looking at Devin count his money in the rearview mirror, with disbelief in her eyes.

Crisi even turned in her seat and looked at Devin in disbelief. They knew Devin had to be young, like high school young, but neither Jackie nor Crisi could believe the young hustler they were crazy about was only in Jr. High School. Devin raised his hands in the air like he was being held up, with money all over his lap, as the two beautiful women stared at him.

"What? You looking at me like you saw a ghost. So, what I'm only fourteen! Age ain't nothing, but a number. Money don't care how old you are," Devin stated, in an authoritative tone.

Wow! You right because you're more mature and you make more money than most of the dudes our age. Damn! You are only fourteen?" Crisi said, her voice caught in her throat.

Jackie had driven the route that Devin hoped she would, down 20th Street. He noticed his mom was not back home yet. His house was dark, and his mom's boyfriend's car was not there when they passed by. Devin hated that he took Jackie by their earlier. He didn't like people knowing where he lived and hoped she wouldn't remember.

"It's been fun, y'all be safe tonight," Devin said, readying himself to get out as Jackie was pulling up to the curb. One thing that getting robbed in the Spencers had taught Devin, was to always be on point. Devin checked himself and his surroundings again, before opening his door to get out.

"What you not going to ask us to come in? You still gonna let me lay it out for you?" Jackie asked, while turning the car off. "Come on girl! I told Devin we would help him get furniture and stuff for his apartment." Jackie got out of the car.

"His apartment?" Crisi asked in a surprised tone, getting out of the car joining Jackie and Devin on the sidewalk, outside Devin's unit in the projects.

"I thought you said y'all was in a rush?" Devin asked, unlocking the front door. When Devin opened the door, the loud smell of marijuana hit him in the nose first, then he focused in on a startled Jamarl and Chuck. He had opened the door so quietly that neither of them heard him come in. They talked about what they would buy with their money, sitting on the floor in the corner, puffing on a kush blunt.

"What's up?" Devin said, walking into the living room, with Jackie and Crisi right behind him.

"What's up with you, homie? It looks like you got the best hand," Chuck said, looking at Crisi and Jackie. *Damn they fine*, Chuck thought to himself.

Devin introduced everybody. "Crisi – Jackie! These are my potnas, Jamarl and Chuck. Chuck – Jamarl! This is Crisi and Jackie."

"What's up y'all?" Vincent said, walking into the living room from the kitchen, eyes locked on Crisi's sexy frame.

"We just came through to check out the spot. Give us a tour Boo," Jackie said. *I can't believe I called him Boo in front of everyone*, Jackie thought to herself.

"Y'all smoke?" Chuck asked, arms stretched out blunt in hand.

"It ain't no bammer is it?" Crisi asked.

"We ain't dem other dudes, you got us confused," Jamarl laughed, a guttural laugh. "We only smoke dat good. This that $700 an ounce shit right here," Chuck passed Crisi the blunt on her way upstairs, behind Jackie and Devin.

"Damn, who are those two bad broads?" Jamarl asked in a low tone.

"That's Devin's homegirls he met in the Spencer Projects. They cool!" Vincent said.

After getting a tour and some good smoke, Jackie and Crisi left high and with a good idea of what kind of furniture they wanted to get for Devin. The apartment only had a living room, kitchen, and two bedrooms. *The space was small, but just how much room did a fourteen-year-old need,* Crisi thought.

∞ ∞ ∞ ∞ ∞ ∞ ∞ ∞ ∞

Jackie and Crisi were in a good mood as they smoked and bopped to the music on their way to the club.

"I can't believe you called Devin Boo," Crisi said, turning the music down.

"I know huh! I had to catch myself cause that shit slipped out. It's just something about him. Every time I see him, he gives me butterflies, that tingle between my legs. No dude has ever made me feel like this, my panties get wet thinking about him. Crisi, he can get it Girl!" Jackie said, in a weary tone.

"Don't trip, I dig him too. He's smooth, and he definitely don't act his age," Crisi said, taking the blunt from Jackie, turning the music back up.

Rrring! Rrring!

"Hello!" Jackie answered her phone, while turning the music down.

"What's up this Devin!"

"I know who it is Boo. Everything alright? What's up?"

"What cha got going tomorrow? Can you pick me up from school? It's Friday, I'm going to need you for a little while again. I gotcha on the gas," Devin said, waiting on an answer.

"That's cool! What time? I don't have to pick Crisi up until 6:00 pm."

"Like 2:45 pm in the parking lot, in the back. Do you know where Norris is?

"I went to Norris," Jackie said.

"Thanks Jackie. It don't sound like you at the club, did you change your mind?"

"No, we just pulled up. We about to go in now."

"Oh...Uh...I'll talk to y'all tomorrow then," Devin said, before hanging up. "Damn! Y'all fools is nosey." Devin's voice reflected loudly in Chuck and Jamarl's direction. They were eavesdropping on his phone conversation, and counting their money on the floor at the same time.

The crew: Devin, Jamarl, Vincent, and Chuck, nailed a curtain over the entrance to the kitchen, so you couldn't see what was going on, but you could still hear. They had a rule in the trap house, that whenever there was more than one of them there, they would alternate serving fiends and nobody who wasn't in the crew, could serve in their spot, and today was Vincent's day.

"Yo V! I'm about to head out," Devin said, grabbing his bike out of the corner. "I'll holler at y'all in the morning."

"See you in the morning D," Vincent yelled from the kitchen.

"Be safe Homie," said Chuck.

"Hey, bring me something in the morning, I'll be done with this," Jamarl said to Devin, as he walked him to the door, so he could lock it behind him.

"I gotcha, y'all be safe," Devin said, getting on his bike headed home.

Chapter 20

The cafeteria at Norris Jr. High School echoed with screams and pandemonium. This was the last day of school and everyone was running wild. It turned out to be a beautiful day outside. The sun shined brightly through the windows in the cafeteria, while the students stood in line to receive a lunch of cheeseburgers and French fries. Jamarl, Devin, Jazz, and Vincent, were standing in the line talking about going to the mall on Saturday and how they couldn't wait to get out of school today, so they could grind when, Jessica walked up.

"What's up Poppi?"

"Damn!" Devin unexpectedly said, not believing he had said it loud, but Jessica looked good in her tight form-fitting Baby Phat jeans jump suit. "What's up J? You didn't get in trouble last night, did you?" Devin asked.

"My brothers are assholes, don't trip! I got them. Did you enjoy your food?"

"Yeah, that shit was bangin!" Devin replied.

"Well, there go my girls, call me some time," Jessica said, passing Devin her phone number on a piece of paper, before she walked off.

"No doubt," Devin responded, as all four of his friend's eyes locked onto Jessica's behind.

"Damn! You better hit that homie," Vincent said. "And stop being scared!"

"Scared! You still ain't fucked Trina, and she been throwing the pussy at you all year."

"You late fool. She came through the trap last night when her mom went to work. I put a blanket on the floor and beat it up. She got that good," Vincent declared. "There go Chuck," Vincent said, waving him over.

"Yo! I need to holla at you D its urgent! What's up V, Jamarl, and Jazz?" Chuck stated in a serious tone.

"What's up Chuck?" Devin asked, his voice now urgent.

Chuck put his arms around Devin's shoulders. "I got the 411 on that boy that robbed you. His name is Mike Mike from up there in the Hilltop Projects. I know where he stays and be at. Gina said her sister fuck wit the fool. He got a trap house over by the Parker Street overpass on 28th Street. What cha wanna do?" Chuck asked.

"See if you can get us a G-ride when we get out of school and let's check it out," Devin said, with a serious tone.

"That's what's up. Hey V! What's up for tonight? You still gonna try to get your sister to rent us some rooms at her job?" Chuck asked.

"What's up y'all?" Trina interrupted. "Vincent you still gonna have that party tonight? My girls said they coming. Devin, Jessica wants to know if you gonna be there?"

"This is the first I have heard about it, but if the crew is in, I'm in," Devin stated, curiously.

"Yeah, it's still on. I'll call you at about 5:00 pm to let you know everything, Trina," Vincent said.

"Trina, is Keisha coming?" Jazz asked.

"Go ask her, you might can get some, if you stop being so scary. Talk to you later," Trina said, before walking off.

"Hey Jamarl, let's go handle this business real quick, and I got that for you," said Devin.

"I'll talk to y'all later," Devin said, leaving the table with Jamarl.

Devin and Jamarl walked to the restroom and waited inside until it was empty of students. After checking all the stalls, making sure there was no one inside, Devin reached inside his back pocket and pulled out an ounce, and gave it to Jamarl.

"I don't have any money on me!" Jamarl said, putting the ounce inside his backpack

"Just give me $900 when you get it," Devin said, headed to class.

"What's up Jazz? Did you talk to Keisha?" Devin asked, sitting at the desk next to Jazz.

"Yeah! She said she's coming, but I don't know how I'm gonna get there," said Jazz.

"Holla at Vincent or Chuck! It's the first Friday, so I'm gonna be grindin. I don't know what time I am going."

"Hey Devin, let me ask you a question."

"What's up Jazz?"

"Why you hustling that dope? You not scared of getting killed or going to jail?"

"Jazz, I'm tired of my mom struggling, tired of coming home to no lights or heat, and I am tired of wearing these same old clothes over and over."

"You still look fresh. You not bummy lookin or nothin, why you trippin?"

"The only reason you not trippin Jazz, is because you get new shit all the time. Y'all lights and shit is always on. You got your mom, dad, grandma, and grandpa. It's just me and my mom Homie. That's why I do what I do. You feel me?"

"Yeah, I guess."

"Whateva Homie! Ima do me and you do you!" Devin stated in an agitated tone.

Chapter 21

"Damn! It's 2:30 pm already," Devin said to himself. He had been spitting game at Jessica for over twenty minutes. Devin knew that he had her open by the way she smiled, giggled, and crossed her legs over and over. She had given him the green light in so many words, letting him know that he could fuck tonight. Devin shifted his dick to the side, so his hard on for Jessica wouldn't be visible, when he stood up.

"Hold on for a sec, I gotta use the restroom," Devin said to Jessica, before getting up to grab the restroom pass off the teacher's desk. Once in the restroom, Devin made sure it was empty. Then he went in a stall, locked the door, and pulled out his phone to call Jackie. He dialed her number and listened as her phone rang several times.

The sound of music was the first thing Devin could hear, before Jackie turned the music down to say "Hello".

"Where you at?" Devin asked.

"Outside in the parking lot." Jackie answered, exhaling smoke from her cigarillo, at the same time.

"That's what's up! I'll be out in a minute." Devin closed his phone and headed back to class.

Devin returned the hall pass, grabbed his backpack, told Jessica he would see her later, and crept out of class a couple minutes before it ended, because he wanted to be outside before the bell rang. Devin checked the hall and parking lot to make sure the coast was clear, then he went out the back exit. He spotted Jackie's car and ran to get inside, throwing his backpack in the backseat, and unconsciously kissing Jackie on the cheek.

Devin reclined his seat all the way back, so he couldn't' be seen from outside.

"What's up Boo? No more school, I know you happy," said Jackie.

"You know it! Now I can get this money 24-7," Devin declared.

"Boo, I need to make one stop before we head north. I gotta meet Pam at Nebraska Furniture Mart."

"That's what's up, let me hit that," Devin said, reaching for the cigarillo in Jackie's hand.

"I didn't know you smoked," Jackie said, passing the cigarillo to Devin.

"I don't, but today is a special day," Devin replied, puffing on the cigarillo. "This is some good shit!" Devin exclaimed, feeling the marijuana relax him as he laid back in his seat. "Ahhh," Devin exhaled the smoke clouds out of his mouth and nose, before taking another puff.

"Northern Lights! It's some good smoke, but not as good as that kush, your homies had," Jackie said, receiving the cigarillo back from Devin.

"I think I know where they got that kush from. I'll get us some when we get to the hood," said Devin.

"That's cool because I only have a corner of this left," Jackie replied, passing the marijuana back to Devin, pulling into the lot of the giant furniture and appliance store, and parking. "You coming in?"

"Nah! I'm cool," Devin said, feeling good off the weed.

"I'll be right back," Jackie said, grabbing her Gucci bag and getting out of the car.

Devin watched Jackie walk through the parking lot. He like the way she walked in her high heels and tight jeans. It was like she was gliding on

Rip the Runway, with her hips switching from left to right and right to left until she entered the store. Reclining back in his seat, Devin puffed on what was left of the cigarillo, until it burned his finders. It was like Devin was floating on cloud nine, daydreaming about getting money, pussy, and the business he needed to take care of with this Mike Mike character.

Rrring! Rrring!

Devin's phone rang, bringing him out of the haze filled daydream. "Hello!"

"Boo, what's the address to your spot in the projects?" Jackie asked.

"Um, 2050 N. 20th Street," Devin answered curiously.

"Ok," Jackie said before hanging up. Five minutes later she was coming out the door with a piece of paper in her hand and a man in hot pursuit on her heels.

Something wasn't right to Devin, so he jumped out of the car and started walking towards Jackie. As Devin got closer, he noticed who the man was that was following behind Jackie. It was RIP, an older dude he knew of from the neighborhood. It appeared that RIP was about to attack Jackie, until he looked up and noticed Devin approaching.

"What's poppin RIP?" Devin spoke to the crazy, strange, and deranged looking man.

RIP looked bad. His eyes were yellowish and red, his clothes were wrinkled and soiled, and he had a dangerous look about his ashy face, like he hadn't slept in days.

"Wha...What's up Little Homie," RIP stuttered, as a startled Jackie turned to see the crazy looking man standing close behind her. "You holdin Little Homie?" RIP's yellow bugged eyes appeared to be scanning Devin's pockets.

"Nah!" Devin stated aggressively. His conscious was telling him something wasn't right with RIP. "Catch me later in the hood, and I'm gonna bless you O.G.! Let's go," Devin turned and said to Jackie.

"Damn, what's wrong with that niggah? He scared the shit out of me!" Jackie looked back over her shoulder at RIP.

"Probably strung out, high off that shit, ain't no telling what that niggah was about to try to do, or what he is gonna do out here." Devin watched RIP walk through the parking lot, looking into the windows of the empty cars.

"Here's your receipt. They are gonna deliver your furniture tomorrow and you have to be there. What time does it say for delivery on your receipt?" Jackie was still shook up from her encounter with RIP, as she looked in the ash tray for the marijuana.

"Says between 10:00 am and noon for delivery."

"Damn niggah, you smoked up all of the cigarillo? You could have at least rolled another one."

"This is a lot of shit, four thousand six hundred twenty-four dollars." Devin read the total on the receipt, trying to picture everything that Jackie had just bought. "Who you think I am, Big Meech or something? I was trying to get a little something for the trap, not go broke. What's this gonna cost me?"

"Don't trip, Pam hooked me up. She had just gotten some new numbers on a couple large limit credit cards, and she's been owing me some cash for a while. She looked out for me, and I looked out for you. If I got a hook up, you got a hook up. You said you was gonna let me decorate your spot, so let me do me."

"How much I owe?" Asked Devin again.

"Just give me two thousand when you got it. I ain't trippin, I gotcha Boo," Jackie said, with a quick kiss to Devin's jaw, that surprised him and her.

"Whoa Shawty! You tryna start something you can't finish. Be careful now!" Devin said, reaching into his front pocket, pulling out a large, folded roll of money. "Watch the road, don't watch me." Devin counted out two stacks and gave the money to a surprised, but impressed Jackie, then shoved the rest of the large roll of bills, back into his pocket.

"You don't have to give it to me yet, I…"

"Well, I got it now, spend it to make some more. That's how the game goes," Devin said, cutting Jackie short. "On my hood!"

"Boy you are something else," Jackie stated with admiration.

"Let's stop in the mall real quick Jac." Devin noticed the Crossroads Mall to his left. "I need to get them new Jordan's that came out today, and some gear to wear to the party tonight."

"What party you going to?"

"My homeboy's sister is throwing a party tonight, a fresh out of school bash. So, I gotta be fresh."

"Well, you can celebrate with me and Crisi tomorrow, when we get back from out of town. We leaving a little later when Crisi gets off work." Jackie drove through the westside parking lot, looking for somewhere close to an entrance. "Devin what size clothes you wear?"

"32-36 with a medium shirt," Devin said, as Jackie parked the Maxima. "Jac pop the trunk so I can put this backpack in it."

The weather was a lot warmer than what the weatherman had forecast, and the sun was beaming down. Devin pulled off the starter jacket he borrowed from Jazz, and placed it in the trunk with his backpack.

Jackie and Devin entered the mall joyously, like a couple. The mall was loudly packed with school kids of all ages, mostly high school kids who had probably left school early. "I need to stop in here first." Devin pointed to Foot Locker.

"I'm gonna go to Dillards. I will meet you in the food court at Orange Julius in thirty minutes." Jackie and Devin parted ways.

Devin walked into Foot Locker feeling like a kid on Christmas. He had never been in a position where he could afford whatever he wanted in Foot Locker. He was stuck gazing at all the shoes on the wall, until he heard some kids talking about the new Jordan's. Devin followed the voices, and they led him to the display of the new Jordan's that had a crowd around them. He walked over and joined the crowd.

"Wow! If I was rich, I would buy all the Jordan's."

"Those are the hardest Jordan's ever."

"Damn, two-hundred dollars?"

Everybody in the crowd had something to say about the new Jordan's, as they stared at the display.

Bzzz! Bzzz! Bzzz! Devin's phone vibrated in his pocket.

"What's poppin?"

"What happened to you? Where you at my hitta?" Vincent asked, over the loud excitement on the bus.

"I had to take care of some shit with Jackie. Man, she got us all kinds of furniture and shit for the trap, bedroom sets, couches, chairs, a stereo, an aquarium, a microwave, and even some TVs like Taco's," Devin boasted.

"Can I help anyone?" Asked the man in the striped referee shirt.

"How? Where you at now my niggah?" Vincent asked, hearing the voice in the background.

"At the Crossroads in Foot Locker. These new J's are sick."

"That's brazy, pick me up a pair, I'll pay you back when you get to the hood"

"What size?"

"Eight and a half or nine my niggah."

"I gotcha my niggah. Yo!" Devin got the salesman's attention, before he walked off.

"Can I help you?"

"Yeah, let me get these Jordan's in a size eight and a half and a size nine."

"A size eight and a half and a size nine?" The salesman asked with doubt in his voice.

"Yes, eight and a half and nine, and let me get a pair of those, and them right there in a size nine also," Devin pointed to the Airforces on the wall.

The salesman walked off to retrieve all the shoes Devin wanted, in doubt that the young black kid could seriously afford this order. Devin browsed around the store, until he noticed the salesman returning with a stack of shoeboxes.

"Would you like to try these on?"

"Just the size nines," Devin said, slipping off his chucks.

A small crowd formed around Devin like he was some kind of superstar, as he tried on the Jordan's. He even noticed two fine teenage girls eyeing him from afar on the low.

So, this is what it feels like to have money, Devin thought to himself, loving all the attention. It felt like a dream to Devin, as he reflected back to always being teased about being poor. It was just the other day he was being joked on about his gear. "This niggah got one pair of shoes and two pair of pants. He done washed these Converses so many times, they just verses," said one kid. "Broke ass niggah," said another.

Devin was always being joked on about his gear, but he wore his clothes with pride and did his best to look fresh in what his mom had purchased, even though he didn't like them. He said nothing because he knew his mom worked hard for everything they had, and he never wanted to hurt her feelings.

"Is everything ok?" The salesman brought Devin back to the present time, Devin's time to shine.

"I'll take 'em all, but I'm gonna keep these on," Devin said, of the Airforce Ones he had tried on last.

Bzzz! Bzzz! Devin's phone vibrated, as he laced up his shoes.

"Hello!"

"What's up Homie?" Asked the familiar voice. "This the homegirl T. You still on? I need to see you."

"No doubt, where you at homegirl?" Devin asked, following the salesman to the cash register.

"Will that be cash or debit?" The salesman interrupted.

"Cash!" Devin replied, pulling the large roll of money out of his pocket. "My bad T, where you say you at?" Devin said, talking back into his phone.

"I'm at the house on 21st and Pratt, 2110 Pratt Street, but I can meet you somewhere."

"That's ok. I am mobile, but I am at the mall right now. I'll be north in about thirty minutes."

"I'll be outside on the porch," Tina said before hanging up.

Devin hung up the phone and looked at the total on the cash register, while noticing in the mirror behind it, that one of the teenage girls was still checking him out. Stimulated by all the stares he was getting, Devin flashed the large roll of money, counting out the total for his purchase. "Let me get that Cincinnati Reds new era fitted cap also," Devin said, putting on a show in front of the full-length mirror, trying on the cap to see how well it matched the shoes and his gear.

"Looks good with those shoes," the salesman said. "I'll throw the hat in for free. Your total is $535."

"$400, $420, $440, $460, $510, $530, $535." Devin counted the money, then handed it to the salesman.

"Would you like the receipt, or do you want it in the bag?"

"You can put the receipt in the bag. I'll take the cap because I'm gonna wear it now," Devin said, as the salesman handed him two large bags.

When Devin turned around the two teenage girls locked eyes with him. The finest one smiled and blushed a little bit before turning away, which gave Devin the confidence he needed to approach them.

"What's up with y'all Shawty? My name is Devin. I was gonna just walk out the store and not speak, but I thought to myself, *I probably will never see these beautiful women again*, so here I am. I gotta go, but I would love to see you again," Devin said, not talking to either girl in particular, but holding out his number on a piece of paper.

"Hi, my name is Stacy, and this is my homegirl Pam," the finest of the two said smiling, as she took the number from Devin's hand.

"I gotta go, call me!" Devin said smiling, walking out the store with a brand-new swag. Once in the crowded halls, Devin shuffled along with the rest of the shoppers. There were a lot of new urban stores that Devin noticed, and he made a note to himself to check them out next time. "Damn, it's some fine girls in here." Devin scanned the halls of the mall going up the escalator, to the food court.

When Devin got upstairs, he scanned the food court looking for Jackie. "Wow," little momma," Devin said when he noticed the thick redbone switching her ass through the mall, sucking on a lollipop. Devin froze watching her every move, until he noticed Jackie standing in line at Orange Julius. He crept up behind Jackie, placed his arms around her waist, and whispered in her ear. "What's your name beautiful?"

Jackie was startled at first, until she recognized Devin's voice. She felt so good in his arms and she could feel his manhood pressed up against her. "I'm here with my man, he's not gonna like you all up on me like this." Jackie played along.

"Fuck him! Do you like it?" Devin teased, with a soft kiss and his tongue on the tip of her ear.

"Mmm yesss!" Jackie said, grinding her ass back into the bulge in Devin's pants.

"You gonna tell me your name Shawty?" Devin asked, as his hands played down from her waist across her zipper.

"Yeesss!" She smiled, weakly shaking her aroused body out of Devin's grasp. "Boy you play too much," Jackie said, in a sensuous tone. "You want something?" She turned and asked.

Devin laughed, then grabbed the four bags Jackie had. "Yeah, get me a large Orange Julius."

"I thought you said you was coming to get a pair of Jordan's?" Jackie teased, looking at all the bags Devin was carrying.

"I know you ain't talking. Look at all these bags."

"Two of 'em are yours, I can take 'em back."

"No, don't do that." Devin smiled, while looking in the bags as they walked.

"Watch where you going, before you run into somebody. It ain't nothing, but some shirts, pants, and cologne."

"Come on let's go, my phone been blowing up," Devin said, pulling his vibrating phone out of his pocket. "Hello!"

"What's up Potna? When you coming through?" Asked Lil Chris.

"I'm on my way. Give me about fifteen minutes."

"That's what's up," Lil Chris stated happily, before hanging up.

Chapter 22

"Damn, it's hot out here," Jackie said, unlocking the door and popping the trunk with the remote. Devin placed the bags in the trunk, then grabbed his backpack, before getting in the car.

"Here roll this up," Jackie said, throwing a box of cigarillos and the corner bag of marijuana into Devin's lap.

"I can't roll," Devin stated, in a serious tone.

"Here you go then," Jackie said, getting out walking around to Devin's side.

Devin hopped over into the driver's seat, then shifted the seat back until he was comfortable. As Devin was driving through the lot, he noticed the two girls from Foot Locker getting in a Chrysler 300.

"Make a left onto 72nd Street," Jackie called out to Devin, pushing send on her phone. "Hey, meet me at Bakers on 72nd," Jackie said, before hanging up and dialing another number, then passing the cigarillo to Devin.

Devin drove down 72nd Street relaxed. The excitement of being behind the wheel had played out. He cruised and puffed on the cigarillo, while Jackie continued to make phone calls.

"Pull up next to that grey truck," Jackie pointed into the Bakers grocery store parking lot up ahead.

Devin pulled in next to the truck and parked while Jackie rolled down her window. The man in the truck got out and came over to Jackie, tossing a wad of bills through the window into her lap. Jackie handed the man something out of her purse, then rolled the window up. Devin was about to put the car into drive and pull off, until Jackie motioned for him to hold on. She took a long puff on the cigarillo, passed it to Devin, then got out of the car. A white Mercedes Benz pulled up and Jackie got in. Devin didn't know what to do when the Mercedes pulled off, with Jackie still inside.

Bzzz! Bzzz! Devin's phone vibrated on his lap.

"Hello," Devin answered, while putting the cigarillo out in the ashtray.

"I need you D! It's rollin! I got money lined up for you, you want it or what?" Tina boldly stated.

I'm on my way, give me about five minutes!" Devin said, patiently waiting for Jackie to pull back up, when another car pulled up alongside him and let the window down. It was an older white man who was trying to see through the tinted windows of Jackie's car. Devin didn't know what to do so he just stayed reclined back in his seat. He noticed the Mercedes pulling back up. Jackie got out, hopped in the car with the white man, and got right back out. As soon as Jackie got in and closed the door, Devin pulled off.

"I gotta go get this money," he told Jackie, turning out of the grocery store's parking lot, headed down Ames Street. Jackie grabbed the blunt out of the ashtray and fired it up, reclining back in her seat as she puffed and inhaled the strong smoke from the Northern Lights marijuana. *It's like a car show out here,* Devin thought to himself, noticing all the custom cars with big rims, nice paint jobs, TVs, and loud music, cruising up and down Ames Street. "I gotta get me something nice!" He said out loud, looking at the Dodge Magnum on 24-inch rims, next to them at the red light.

"Yeah, that's nice," Jackie said, as she leaned back into her seat, after looking at the car. "Do you know what you want?" She asked.

"Not yet, I gotta get my money up."

"We can go check some car lots out when I get back tomorrow, if you want to"

"I'm cool, let me get my money right first."

Devin could see Tina's car on the street after he turned down Pratt. Then he saw her walking off the porch when she noticed the Maxima. Devin pulled up in front of her house and was about to get out, until he noticed all the strange faces, except for B Mac's. He let the window down and spoke to B Mac, then motioned for Tina to get in.

"What the business is Homegirl?"

"Let me get three of 'em Homie. I'll call you later when I get finished with mine. These are for the homeboys."

"I hope you getting yours off this, because they go for $1200 all day in the hood," Devin said, handing Tina the three ounces out of his backpack.

"You already know it." Tina smiled, giving Devin three stacks of rubber banded money. "That's a thousand in each stack," Tina stated in a serious tone, as she watched Devin count the money. "Holla at cha in a minute D," she said, getting out the car, glancing over at Jackie, before she closed the door.

"That bitch would be fire, if she took off all those baggy ass man clothes," Jackie said, seriously.

"I need to go to the Spencers before we go get some of the kush y'all was smoking last night," Devin said, dialing Lil Chris's number into his phone, and pushing the send button. Devin listened, as Chris's phone rang several times with no answer. He hung up, then dialed Vincent's number.

"Talk about it!" Vincent answered his phone on the first ring.

"What's up Potna?"

"Shit! Getting this money. Yo! You get them Jordan's for me?" Vincent asked in a weary tone.

"Yeah, I got 'em for you. Check it though, I need some of that good y'all was smoking last night," Devin said, his voice urgent.

"We got that shit from J-Low. I just called him twenty minutes ago. He's suppose to be coming by here. You want me to grab you something? I got that money for the shoes and that other," Vincent declared.

"Yeah, grab me a zone 1. I'll be through there in a minute."

"Ok! Oh yeah, Chuck said he got that ride."

"Tell him to hold tight. I will be there in a minute." Devin pulled into the Spencer Projects. He grabbed an ounce and his pistol out of his backpack. I'll be right back Shawty," Devin said, tucking the gun under his shirt and placing the dope in his pocket, before he got out.

The weather was nice, and the projects were alive and buzzing with people all over. Devin noticed a group of girls staring at him, as he walked up the sidewalk to Bo's. Some were giggling and some were smiling. He could tell they were talking about him, so he waved at them, and they giggled, blushed, and waved back. Devin smiled at them, then walked into Bo's.

"What's up Potna," Lil Chris greeted Devin first.

"What's up with y'all? You look like somebody died," Devin said to Bo.

"I think I'm coming down with something," said Bo.

"Let me holla at cha real quick Lil Chris," Devin said, walking into the kitchen.

"What's up?" Chris asked, walking into the kitchen behind Devin.

"Here," Devin said, pulling the ounce out of his pocket, then giving it to Lil Chris. "Make sure you take care of Bo for me. Just give me $1,000 dollars off that ounce."

"I'll probably be ready tomorrow. I'm grindin all night," Lil Chris barked. "Oh yeah, my relative is trying to cop an ounce too."

"Where he at? I gotta bounce?"

"Hold on, he's next door," Chris said, on his way to go get his relative.

"Tell him $1200 for an onion," Devin said, headed out the door behind Chris. He had to run back to the car to grab the ounce out of his backpack. Devin was happy he decided to bring six ounces to school with him today. He watched everything around him again, running back into Bo's. When he got inside there was a jet-black lanky kid standing next to Lil Chris counting some money. "Where Bo go?" Devin asked.

"He went upstairs to lay down."

"Here you go, $1200," the lanky kid said, handing Devin the stack of bills. "If it's that A-1, I'm gonna be hooking back up with you real soon.

"That's what's up! Just have Lil Chris get at me when you're ready, because it's A-1." Devin handed the lanky kid the dope. "What's your name?"

"Lil Rod!"

"They call me D. Yo, I'll holla at cha later Lil Chris. Hold it down for me," Devin said, before he ran back to the car.

Chapter 23

Vincent was the only one at the spot when Devin and Jackie walked in. "Damn homie, you buy the whole mall?" Vincent asked, after he saw all the bags in Devin's hands.

"Nah, here you go," Devin said, handing Vincent the box of Jordan's marked size 8 ½.

"That's what I'm talking about. These motha fuckas are nice. I like dem one's you got on too D." Vincent said happily, while checking his potna out.

"Yeah, I had to have 'em when I seen 'em."

"What else you got?"

"These khaki-colored Airforce Ones," Devin replied, lifting them up out the shoe box. "And Jackie got me some…". Devin paused, pulling the clothes Jackie had gotten for him out of three sacks. Jackie had purchased Devin two Roca Wear jeans outfits and some Sean John jeans shorts with Sean John shirts to go with them.

"Don't forget the Sean John "Unforgivable Cologne", Jackie said, grabbing the cologne out the bag, and spraying some on Devin's neck. "Mmm, this smells so good," Jackie said. "Always remember, women like dudes that smell good."

"I would hit the mall up today, but I need to get everything situated for this party tonight. What cha gonna do D?" Vincent asked.

"I'm trying to figure out how I'm gonna get there, because I am really trying to get this money. But I'm gonna be there even if I have to catch a jitney cab.

"You don't have to catch no cab Boo, me and Crisi gonna rent a car to go out of town. So, you can keep the Max while we are gone, if you want to."

"What time are y'all leaving?" Asked Devin.

"We gonna leave at about 7:00 pm and be back early tomorrow morning."

"What the business is? What y'all got poppin in this spot?" Chuck interrupted, coming in from the kitchen door. "Here goes your key back. I haven't seen Jamarl to give him his," Chuck said to Vincent, who had given Chuck his key to get two duplicates made for him and Jamarl.

"So, when are y'all gonna pick up the rental," Devin asked Jackie.

"Right after I pick Crisi up from work. They have an Avis out by her job. Why what's up?"

"Nothing, I need to go take care of something. That's all."

"Are you ready? I can take you. I don't have to pick Crisi up until 6:00 o'clock."

"I'm cool, I don't need no ride," Devin lied. "Just call me after you pick Crisi up."

"Ok!"

"Chuck you ready? Let's handle this," Devin stated, in a serious tone.

"Hold on, I'm going!" Vincent barked.

"Nah, stay here and hold the spot down. It's the first, somebody needs to be here."

"Don't trip, we got this," Devin boldly stated, as him, Chuck, and Jackie walked out the front door.

"Holla at me later Sexy," Devin said, as he watched Jackie walk to her car.

"Be careful," Jackie turned and said to Devin, not liking the look that she had seen on his face, while he was talking to Chuck. It was like he transformed into someone else.

"Come on, the car is in the back," Chuck said.

Chapter 24

"That's suppose to be his spot right there," Chuck said, pointing at the big house on the hill.

"Look at all the traffic going in and out," Devin said, turning off Parker Street onto 28th Street. He drove by the house a couple of times, circling the block.

"You think he in there? What cha wanna do?" Chuck asked, undecided.

"Let's check it out for a minute," Devin said, parking the car down the street where they could watch the house without being seen. Sitting low in their seats, Chuck and Devin watched the house as fiend after fiend, entered and exited, but still no sign of Mike Mike.

"Fuck this, let's just rush up in that Bitch, blastin," Chuck said, tired of waiting.

"We ain't on no dumb shit like that. We don't know how many people are in there or what they got. They could..., hold on, that looks like that fool right there, coming down the stairs with that gym bag!" Devin pointed. "Yeah, that is that fool!" Devin said, slowly pulling out from behind the car he had parked behind. Devin was following behind Mike Mike when Mike Mike finally turned around, eyes like a deer in headlights.

"He spotted us," Chuck said. "Shit there he goes!"

Devin spun the steering wheel hard to the left. The Nova skidded toward a stop sign, then hopped the curb with a jolting thud. Chuck and Devin jumped out and started to run after Mike Mike.

"We got your ass now!" Devin yelled.

Devin and Chuck shot down a narrow, twisted alley behind Mike Mike, who was suppose to be one of the dudes who robbed Devin in the Spencers. They were a lot younger than Mike Mike, but more thorough, at least in their minds they were.

"Oh," Chuck huffed, matching Devin stride for stride. "We're good for the long haul, just don't let him make it to the projects."

Sweat was already forming on Devin's neck and back. The perspiration was dripping down from his braids, burning his eyes. "We got his ass now," Devin said, as he accelerated, turning up the projects, gaining on Mike Mike who looked back and couldn't believe they were right behind him. Two freight trains on his tail and there was no way for him to get off the track.

Chuck had put it in full gear and Devin gave it everything, still matching Chuck step for step. It was like they were having their own private foot race and Mike Mike was the finish line. They both hit him at the same time. Mike Mike went down hard, rolled a few times, moaned, and then looked up in total amazement.

"God damn! Who are y'all? What did I do?"

Smack!

"Shut your punk ass up. You know what you did," Devin said, smacking Mike Mike across the face with the pistol again, knocking blood from his mouth.

Scared to death, finally realizing who Devin was, Mike Mike started telling everything from who all was in on robbing him in the Spencers, to who had been doing the shootings in the hood.

Devin gripped his gun angrily. "Fuck, you think I was some young punk or something? Huh? You think you gonna rob me, bust my head, then walk around like it ain't nothing, fool? You must really take me for soft!"

Mike Mike was truly scared. He realized there was no way he could get out of this, so he begged and snitched with his arms wrapped around the gym bag like a pillow. "Pl... ple... please, I already told you who made me rob you and who been doing all the shootings in y'all hood, please..."

The first blast from Devin's gun cut his sentence short and blew a chunk out the side of Mike Mike's head.

"Damn!" Chuck hollered, surprised at what had just taken place.

"It's broad daylight fool," Chuck said nervously.

"I don't give a fuck!" Devin said through clenched teeth, as he surveyed the area, making sure there were no witnesses.

BOK! BOK!

"We in this together!" Chuck replied, coldly pumping two shots into Mike Mike's chest.

Devin looked at Mike Mike's lifeless body and grabbed the gym bag from around his shoulders, before running back to the car with Chuck on his heels.

Devin jumped back in the car and laid the pistol on his lap. "We gotta get rid of this car," he said to Chuck as they cruised back down the hill.

"I know a place, the dead end across 16th, but we need some gas!" Chuck said, still in shock.

Devin pulled in an alley near his house and parked. "Let's see what's in this bag. Damn!" Devin said to Chuck., when he unzipped the bag and noticed all the loose cash.

"Wow, how much you think it is," Chuck asked.

"I don't know, come on! We can count it at my house. I think we got a gas can that we use for the lawn mower. Can't nobody see the car back here," Devin said, wiping the car down before he got out.

"Them fools getting money in that spot," Chuck said, wiping his side of the car down, before getting out to catch up to Devin, who had taken off in a slow jog down the alley already.

Once inside the house, Devin made sure that his mom wasn't home, before dumping the money out onto the floor in his room.

"Swwizzz," Chuck whistled. "That's a lot of money."

"Don't just stand there, fool! Help me count it."

It took Devin and Chuck about twenty minutes to count all the money. They both stared in amazement at the big pile on the floor.

"How much you count?" Devin asked Chuck.

"$8240," Chuck said smiling.

"We came up Homie! I counted $10,810," said Devin. "That's almost twenty racks."

"Hell yeah!" Chuck said, smiling ear to ear. Devin split the money and handed Chuck his half. "Come on let's go get rid of this car," Chuck said, pushing his half of the money roughly into his front pockets.

"Hold on let me get some clothes together for tonight," Devin said, opening the drawer to get a pair of socks and boxer shorts, while putting the money in the same drawer under some clothes. "Make sure you change out of those clothes too," Devin said to Chuck on their way downstairs.

"I was gonna throw all this shit away as soon as we got back to the hood.

"The gas can is in the backyard," Devin said, locking the door."

Chapter 25

The dead end off 16th Street was a secluded wooded area by the railroad tracks. With the sun now gazing down, it would be nearly impossible for anyone to see Devin and Chuck dousing the stolen car in gasoline.

"Look around and make sure we didn't drop nothing. I'm about to light this bitch up," Devin said, throwing the gas can into the front seat.

"Everything's cool! Come on let's go," Chuck said, as the interior started to flame up.

Chuck and Devin were on 18th Street when they heard the car explode into flames.

"So, do you think that fool was telling us the truth about who shot up Tray's funeral, and killed Jamarl's brother?"

"No doubt! I could see it in his eyes, he was scared to death," Devin answered.

"Well, all dem fools gonna get paid a visit," Chuck said, with a cold calmness.

"I can't believe that fool snitched out his homies. I would never do that to y'all. Ima take mine like a gangsta. If you gonna kill me, then kill me. Don't be swisher sweet crying and snitchin. Be a…"

Bzzz! Bzzz!

Devin reached into his pocket to grab his phone, "Hello!"

"What's up Boo? Where you at? We got the rental, but we needed to make a couple stops. Are in a rush now?" Jackie inquired, as her voice riddled with anxiety.

"I'm at the spot in the hood."

"Good! We are crossing Dodge by Central, so we will be pulling up in a minute. Be looking out for us," Jackie said, before hanging up.

Devin and Chuck made it to 20ᵗʰ Street at the same time Jackie and Crisi had pulled in front of the spot.

Bzzz! Bzzz! Devin's phone rang.

"I'm right behind you!" Devin said, walking up to the rented Chevy Impala Crisi was driving, knocking on her window, then hanging up his phone.

"Boy!" Crisi said startled, then smiling weakly. "You scared the shit out of me," Crisi said, getting out of the car to give Devin a hug.

"Come on with dat family reunion shit, we gotta go bitch," Jackie said, getting out of the Maxima and handing Devin the keys, before opening up the passenger door on the Impala to get in.

"What? No love!" Devin said, playfully holding his arms out for Jackie.

"Boy pleeeaaasse…" Jackie walked over to give Devin a quick hug and a soft peck on the lips. "Crisi got y'all a housewarming gift, it's in the backseat," Jackie said, getting in the car. "Take care of my baby, I will call you tonight," Jackie said, as Crisi pulled off.

"Wow! You got it like that?" Chuck asked, surprised they had left Devin the Maxima.

Bzzz! Bzzz! Devin's phone rang.

"Hello!" Devin answered, walking into the house.

"Who's that?" Jamarl called from the kitchen, before looking around the curtains.

"What's up D?" Vincent's voice came screaming through Devin's phone.

"Oh, my bad Homie, what's up?" Devin said.

"I'm at the hotel. My sister got us two nice rooms. It's on tonight! Yo, where you at?"

"At the spot!" Devin replied.

"Ask Jamarl if he got the liquor."

"Hold on," Devin said, walking in the kitchen. Jamarl was serving some fiends, but Devin could see all the alcohol on the counter. "Yeah, he got it. Did you get the smoke," Devin asked.

"Yeah! I got you a zip. I put it with the rest of your stuff up in your room. I had Crackhead Wardy put locks on our bedroom doors. Your key is in the bottom drawer in the bathroom. I rented one of the fiend's car for the weekend. I will be back in a minute to pick y'all up."

"I'm cool, I will probably go by and pick Jazz up, after me and Chuck change clothes. I got Jackie's Maxima."

"You go Pimpin," Vincent said laughing.

"Holla at you later," Devin said hanging up. "What's up Jamarl?" Devin spoke, giving him a pound after he got off the phone.

"Same shit Homie, I got half that money for you now," Jamarl said, counting money out on the counter in the kitchen. "Five hundred!" Jamarl said, placing the money into Devin's hands.

"Yo!" Chuck said, coming into the kitchen. "I'm about to go home and change. Anybody heard from V?"

"Yeah, he said he would be back through to pick y'all up later on."

"You gonna hold it down Jamarl?" Chuck asked.

"Yeah! I'm already dressed. I got this," Jamarl replied, letting another fiend into the kitchen. "What cha need?" Jamarl asked.

"Let me holla at you Chuck," Devin said, wrapping his arms around Chuck's shoulders, as they walked out the door. "Thanks! That was good looking out today," Devin stated, in a sincere tone.

"Don't trip Homie! Like I said, we in this together."

"That's what's up," Devin said, going back to the house, walking past the fiends that Jamarl had just served.

"I'm about to hop in the shower," Devin said, looking in the bag that Crisi had gotten for him.

"What's that?" Jamarl asked.

"Looks like some stuff for the bathroom," Devin said, pulling a shower curtain, floor rug, toothpaste, toothbrushes, shower gel, deodorant, and some towels out the bag. "Just what I needed. Hold it down Jamarl, I'm going upstairs to take a quick shower." Devin headed upstairs.

After putting the shower curtain up and the rest of the stuff that Crisi purchased for the bathroom away, Devin grabbed the key to his room out of the bottom drawer. When he unlocked his bedroom door and walked in, the loud smell from the bag of kush overwhelmed the small empty room. Devin walked over to the corner his backpack was in and checked his belongings, everything was still there like he expected. He grabbed the bag of marijuana off the floor and placed it into the backpack with the two ounces of dope, then zipped it up. He grabbed the underwear and socks he brought from home out of his pockets, locked his door, and headed for the shower. Devin turned the shower on and got undressed. Before he could get in the shower, he heard his phone vibrating on the floor inside his pants pocket. He thought about ignoring the call, but changed his mind, reaching down, grabbing his phone out his pants, answering in a groggy tone.

"Hello!"

"Young D. How you doing up there?" Taco asked.

"Yo, what's up Taco? Everything's good in the O. I got that put up for you," Devin said, excited to be talking to Taco.

"I was calling to let you know I will be there tomorrow. You said you got that! You done already?" Taco laughed in astonishment.

"Yeah, don't trip, I got ya Big Homie. Call me as soon as you get here."

"R...Right will do, be safe Young D," Taco said, before hanging up.

Devin closed his phone then got in the shower. He closed his eyes and relived the shooting from earlier, lathering up with the Burberry shower gel. Turning the hot water up, Devin stood under the streaming hot water, trying to stop his mind from replaying the scenes of Mike Mike's horrible looking and dead body, every time he closed his eyes. The cold game that Devin was in, had caused him to become a killer at a very young age, and he felt neither regret nor remorse for what he had done. To Devin, it was something that had to be done.

"I need to roll me one up," Devin said to himself, thinking that the kush would help. He turned the water off, grabbed a towel, and headed to his room. "Damn! I can't wait until tomorrow." Devin noticed he had nowhere to sit, so he sat on the floor and laced up his new Jordan's, grabbing the Sean John jeans with the Sean John shirt that matched the new Jordan's. "Yes! Yes!" Devin said, impressed with his new gear and the fact that the days of not being able to afford a pair of Air Jordan's was over.

Once dressed, Devin sprayed on a little of the Unforgivable, grabbed his money and kush, and locked his door before he headed downstairs.

"You got some Swishers?" Devin asked Jamarl, who was sitting on the floor about to listen to a portable CD player.

"Nah, but I will run to the store and get some. I can smell that good!"

"That's cool. I will hold the spot down," Devin said, running upstairs to grab some dope out of his room. On Devin's way back downstairs, someone was already knocking on the backdoor, and his phone was vibrating in the same pocket as the gun he knew he needed to get rid of, but couldn't move himself to do it, until he had another one to replace it.

"What's up?" Devin said, sternly opening the door, staring two fiends in the face.

"Where the other dude at that took care of me last time?" The fiend asked.

"He's not here. It's the same shit, I got what cha need."

"Let me see what you got for a hundred." The fiend stated in an undecided tone.

"What you trying to do Big Man?" Devin asked the other man.

"I'm trying to spend, so if you got that love like homeboy…"

"Here you go," Devin said, breaking off a piece for the hundred, then a fifty piece for the other man.

"Hell yeah," the fiend said, digging in his pockets, pulling out a hundred-dollar bill, high beams still locked on the boulder in Devin's hands. "Here you go Little Homie. Good looking," The fiend said smiling, as him and Devin exchanged money for dope. "What they call you

Little Homie? You got a number? I usually spend more than this. I'm trying to get back on my feet. How much your quarters go for?"

"Three hundred! They call me Lil D," Devin said, giving the other man his dope, before placing the money in his pockets.

"That's love! I'll be back Young D."

"Me too," the other man stated anxiously.

As Devin was letting the two men out, he could see Jamarl coming down the sidewalk, talking to Jerome. Jerome was about eighteen or nineteen. He lived across the street from Charles Drew Health Clinic, on the other side of the ballfield, in the projects. Jerome and the other homie Mac Shawn were hustla-a-holics, they almost never left the hood. Mac Shawn and Jerome had a trap spot at the end of crack alley.

"What's up Rome?" Devin said, greeting Jerome and Jamarl as they walked into the kitchen.

"Tryna get right. I hear you got that good over here," Jerome said with admiration. Jerome had known and watched Vincent and Devin around the hood for a longtime, so when he heard they were in the game, he wasn't really surprised.

"We on our way Homie, "Everyday I'm hustling!" Devin marked Rick Ross. "So, what can I do for you Homie?"

"Two – Three – Four, depends on the ticket," Jerome stated, in a serious tone.

"The lowest I can do right now is stack a piece."

"That's cool! I respect the hustle. Let me get three of 'em."

"Hold on for a minute." Devin ran upstairs to grab his backpack. "I only got two of 'em here," he said, walking back in the kitchen. "But give me a minute and I will bring you one around to your spot. I gotta run and get it," Devin said, placing the dope on the scale.

"Just come by the spot. I don't want to hear Mac Shawn's mouth."

"Give me about fifteen minutes," Devin said, reaching for his phone that was vibrating in his pocket. "Hello!"

"Don't forget Homie," Jerome said, giving a pound to Devin and Jamarl, before leaving.

"Hello!" Devin said, into the phone again.

"What's up D? You still going to V's party?"

"Yeah, I'm going. What's up with you? Are you going?"

"I need V's number, so I can get a ride."

"Don't trip! Are you dressed already?

"Yeah."

"I'll be over in a minute," Devin said, hanging up.

"Yo! Jamarl! Devin yelled, over the loud "Yo Gotti" CD Jamarl had blastin out the CD player, in the living room.

"What's up? You call me?" Jamarl asked, walking into the kitchen.

"You could've heard me, if you didn't have that music blastin. Turn it down a little, so you can hear the door. I am about to go get Jazz; I'll be right back Homie." Devin said, headed back upstairs to put up the dope he had in his backpack. *I might as well leave all this shit,* Devin thought to himself, deciding on not taking the kush or the gun. He tossed the dope and the marijuana on the shelf in his closet, locked his door, and ran back downstairs. "Here Jamarl," Devin said, handing Jamarl the 4-5. "I'll be right back," Devin headed out the backdoor.

Chapter 26

"Devin parked at Dailey's gas station on 16th Street. then walked through the field to Jazz's house. The last thing he needed was for Ms. James or Grandmomma James, to see him driving Jackie's car. "Hi Grandmomma," Devin said, walking onto the porch, Jazz's grandma and grandpa's favorite spot. "Jazz home?"

"Hey Baby, go on inside. He's in there somewhere."

Devin walked back to Jazz's room and opened the door. "What's up fool?" Devin said, walking into Jazz's room. Jazz's room was always neat and everything in order. Low tops, high tops, starter caps hanging on the walls with the NBA posters, PlayStation games, and CD's neatly stacked by the TV and stereo.

"Damn! Look at you fool, new Jordan's and shit." Jazz said, admiring his homeboy's Jordan gear. "I gotta have them,"

"I'm surprised you don't got 'em yet," Devin responded.

"Tomorrow," Jazz smiled. "I told my grandma I was spending the night at your house," Jazz said, in a weary tone.

"That's cool. I'm gonna tell my mom that I am spending the night over here. Let me see the phone." Devin grabbed the phone from Jazz and dialed his home number. He nervously listened as the phone rang.

"Hello!"

"What cha doing Mom?"

"Frying some pork chops for dinner, so bring your ass home."

"Jazz wants me to spend the night. We got a game tomorrow and Grandmomma James is gonna take us. She said I could stay over, but to call and ask you." Devin lied.

"I don't care boy. I guess I can quit cooking?"

"She said I could stay the night!" Devin said out loud to no one, so his mom could hear. "I will be home in a minute. I have to come get my shoes and some clothes." Devin lied.

"Do you want me to finish cooking dinner? Did you eat yet?"

"We ate already." Devin lied again.

"Well, I guess I can get ready to go to work. I'm working at the bar again tonight. If you're not here by the time I leave, look on the table, I will leave some money for you."

"That's ok Mom. We helped Mr. Henderson move, and he gave us twenty dollars a piece. Love you Mom," Devin rushed off the phone. "It's on!" Devin said, handing Jazz back his phone.

"So how we gonna get to V's party?" Asked Jazz.

"I got my girl's Maxima parked at Dailey's."

"Yo girl's Maxima?" Jazz stated, in a surprised tone.

"Just come on fool, let's go!"

Jazz grabbed his backpack and they headed out.

"Bye Grandmomma," the boys said, when they reached the porch.

"Bye Babies!"

"It's on tonight," Devin said, as they walked down Victor Street. "I'm gonna fuck the shit out of Jessica tonight."

"Keisha was talkin like she was wit it earlier. I can't wait fool," Jazz said.

"Come on, let's go into Dunn Deals. I need to give my mom time to leave."

Dunn Deals was a soul food spot on 16th and Victor and Devin loved their bacon double cheeseburger deluxe.

Bzzz! Bzzz! Devin's phone vibrated in his pocket, while they were eating.

"Hello!" Devin answered, with a mouthful of food.

"Where y'all at fool?" Vincent asked.

"Dunn Deals!"

"Trina and them are already at the room waiting on us."

"We will be there in about ten minutes. Let me run by the house real quick."

"Hurry up!" Vincent said, hanging up.

"Come on," Devin said, stuffing the rest of his burger into his mouth, before paying for their food, and leaving a three-dollar tip on the table.

"We need to find somebody to get us a box of Swishers," Devin said, as they walked down the sidewalk to Dailey's.

"We cool! Old girl don't be trippin that's at work now," Jazz said, as they walked into the store.

"Let me get a pack of Swishers, cigarillos, and two boxes of those condoms," Jazz pointed.

The girl stared at them for a minute, then grabbed the Swishers, and the rubbers. "I was wondering when you was gonna come back and get that clean as car," the girl behind the counter said to Devin, as she placed their stuff in the bag. "That will be $9.35."

"Let me get $20 dollars worth of gas too," Devin said, pulling the large wad of money out his pocket to pay.

"Can I help y'all with anything else?" The girl said smiling, flirtatiously grabbing the money out of Devin's hands. "Use pump one," she said, still staring at the sexy chocolate boy in the Jordan's. She liked what she was looking at, and set her mind to check for him again, seeing what he was all about. She liked ballers and this fine young tender sure looked like one, she thought to herself, as she watched him pump his gas. She even waved when they exited out the lot.

"Damn, old girl is all on your dick," Jazz said, noticing the eye contact and the wave from the girl behind the counter.

It only took Devin a couple minutes to run in the house, stash his money, and grab the rest of his dope, before he was back outside and headed to Jerome's.

"Where you headed?" Jazz asked, when he noticed Devin turning onto Paul Street instead of heading to the trap.

"I need to run in here real quick," Devin said, parking in front of Jerome's.

"What's up Homie?" Mac Shawn greeted Devin on the sidewalk with a pound. "Go on in. Jerome is in there waiting on you."

Devin knocked then walked in with Mac Shawn. "Damn Homie, I thought you was fakin. What took you so long?"

"Had to pick up the homie," Devin said, pulling three ounces out his backpack, then handing it to Rome, who put the dope on a scale.

"This shit look A-1!" Rome said, throwing the dope to Mac Shawn.

"Hard white!" Mac Shawn said, looking at the dope in his hands. "D, you got another one on you?" Mac Shawn asked, wanting another one for himself.

"Yeah, here you go," Devin replied, handing Mac Shawn an ounce out his backpack.

"Little Homie we spending good money with you this time cause it's some bullshit going around, but try to get us some better prices and we will at least get a nine piece every time. Fuck wit us and we gonna fuck wit you. We can all get this money Homie." Jerome said, handing Devin the three stacks.

"I hear y'all got a nice trap on the other side. Y'all got some heat?" Mac Shawn asked.

"Yeah, we cool!"

"Be careful Homie, these fools are thirsty out here," Mac Shawn said, giving Devin his money.

"You got a number fool?" Rome asked.

"212-6829," Devin responded, headed out the door. When Devin got outside, Jazz was sitting on the car talking to Sheila and Kim, two girls from school, who lived in the projects.

"What's up Sheila – Kim?" Devin spoke, before getting in the car.

"See y'all later," Jazz said, getting in the car. "Everybody's talking about V's party tonight. I didn't know Soul from the radio station was gonna be the D.J."

"Yeah, his sister hooked him up, V is doing it real big tonight. The radio's been talking about the Jr. High Bash all day," Devin said, pulling in the parking lot, in the back of the trap.

"That little ballroom at the hotel is gonna be packed," Jazz said, walking in the back door, surprising the two fiends and Chuck who was serving them.

"What's up y'all?" Chuck asked.

"What's up?" Devin and Jazz replied.

"What's up Jamarl? What's up Vincent?" Jazz spoke to Jamarl and Vincent, who were in the living room, when they walked in.

"Took y'all long enough," Vincent said, sitting on the floor, rolling a blunt.

"Gotta get this money first," Devin said, headed upstairs to put his dope away, and grab his bag of kush. "Yo V!" Devin called down the stairs for Vincent.

"What's up D?" Vincent asked, running up the stairs.

"You got that money for me? I talked to Taco and they will be here tomorrow."

"Yeah, I was gonna give it to you earlier, but you was gone," Vincent responded, walking out of Devin's room unlocking the door to his room.

"Damn! You done moved all your clothes in here?" Devin said, surprised at all the stuff in Vincent's room.

"This is where I'm gonna live!" Vincent replied. "Somebody needs to be here all the time. My mom don't give a fuck, we hardly ever see each other anyway. My sister has been raising me ever since my mom started fucking wit this crack shit. Homie, shit is crazy! My mom don't come home for like three days after she gets her check, by then there's nothing left to buy groceries. My sister's been paying the bills with her check. That's why we gotta stay on! D, we gotta get paid homie. I gotta take care of my sister. She's gonna be a senior next year and all she talks about is college. Here Homie!" Vincent said, handing Devin the $6,000 dollars. "Homie, this crack shit you plugged us with, is the best thing that could have happened in my life right now," Vincent said seriously. "Look at us Homie! Ashy to classy, and ain't no going back you dig? I don't know about you, but I like my new look," Vincent continued, feeling himself off the kush, and money in his pocket.

Vincent was clean in his Levi's 501 Blue Jeans, new Jordan's, and white t-shirt.

"I feel the same as you do Homie, ain't no turning back. I'm gonna be the best hustler these fools ever seen in the O," Devin said, counting the money. "I've been watching a couple of the older homies hustle for a couple years now. We are laced already Homie. We don't need no iron, we just gotta stay true to each other, loyalty, respect, and honor. No man or woman can ever come between us Homie. I gotcha V! Let's get this money!" Devin said, locking his door.

Jamarl, Jazz, and Chuck already had a blunt going when Vincent and Devin returned back downstairs.

"Hold up! We gonna toast to this night, to the crew," Vincent said, rushing into the kitchen.

"One of y'all show me how to roll one of these," Devin said, reaching in his pockets, pulling out the box of Swisher's.

"Give me one!" Chuck said, pointing to the cigarillo in Devin's hands.

"Take it like this, then push your fingernails, creasing the blunt open down the center like this, gently pulling the Swisher open. Then dump this shit out and lick it a little, until the cigarillo is moist and doesn't crack, fill it up and roll!"

"Here Devin said, giving Chuck a couple of buds of kush to roll," while he rolled his first cigarillo.

"I got this!" Devin said, sealing his blunt closed. "This shit looks professionally rolled." Devin laughed, while holding his blunt in the air for everyone to see.

"Yo! Come get y'all drinks," Vincent called from the kitchen.

"What's this?"

"Ciroc and pineapple, my sister and cousin turned me on to this. It's good. Here comes the toast y'all," Vincent said, holding his glass in the air. "To us, to money!" Vincent toasted.

"Yeah, I like that, because when you see us, you gonna see money," Devin toasted, then took a big gulp of his drink.

"This is good," Jazz said.

"That's what I said when I tasted my sister's. It's on tonight. My sister and my cousin gonna have them high school girls there. They been telling people about this party for a minute, and she was so happy when we gave them the money for the D.J., Mista Soul."

"That fool from the radio station?"

"Yeah, he throws the hottest parties in the city. That's the only reason my sister got us the rooms and we get to come. I've just been telling mutha fuckas I'm having a party, since she told me I could invite some of my friends."

"Fuck a party!" Jamarl said, walking in the kitchen to answer the knock at the door.

"Finish up! We gotta be rollin out. Tina and them blowing my phone up," Vincent said.

"Yo Devin, come here Homie!" Jamarl called from the kitchen. "Here you go." Jamarl passed Devin $500 dollars when he came in the kitchen. "Let me get another one! I'm not going to no party. I'm gonna stay here and get this money."

"It's gonna be a lot of bad bitches, you better come on fool," Devin said.

"M.O.B., money over bitches! Aint' that what you told me?" Jamarl said, waiving the thick stack of bills in his hand.

"Fo sho!" Devin shook his head in agreement. "Hold on, let me run upstairs real quick."

"Hey, sell me some smoke too," Jamarl called behind Devin, who was already headed upstairs.

"You not going?" Vincent asked Jamarl in surprise.

"Man, it's been rolling all day. We might as well let 'em know we gonna be pumpin 24-7 at this bitch. Somebody needs to always hold the spot down."

"True – true! You want my strap?" Asked Vincent.

"Nah! I got Devin's 4-5. I got this y'all, have fun. Ima have fun getting this money."

"Here you go," Devin said, handing Jamarl the ounce of dope and the $50-dollar loud pack. "Give me my $50 bucks fool. I didn't want to sell none of my Kush," Devin said, with a blank expression, holding out his hand for the $50 dollars.

"Be safe J and start looking out the window to see who it is, before you open the door," Chuck said.

"Lock the screen door and keep your heat on you," Devin said, headed out the door with Jazz.

"I got this," Jamarl reassured them.

"I'll be back a little later, so don't lock the front screen door," Chuck said, closing the door behind him.

Chapter 27

Jazz and Devin rode in the Maxima, while Chuck and Vincent rode in a fiends Impala SS. It took long enough for Jazz to roll another cigarillo, (which surprised Devin that Jazz already knew how to do it) for them to smoke before they finally reached the Holiday Inn on 72nd and Grover. When they got upstairs to the room Trina, Jessica, Gina, and Keisha seemed to already be having a party. They had music pumping, drinks, and a blunt blazing.

"What's up y'all?" Devin spoke, checking Jessica out at the same time, while everyone else greeted each other.

"Damn! You look good Mommi," Devin said, sitting down next to Keisha and Jessica on the bed.

All four girls looked like they just came from the mall, but Devin was only checking for Jessica, who had on a Roca Wear shirt and skirt that was like a cheerleading outfit. The skirt hugged her nice butt and the shirt fit just right showing off her sexy body. Devin stared her up her long legs, all the way to the bottom of her skirt and shook his head. Jessica was one bad Spanish chick. They all chilled and had a good time in the room laughing, talking, smoking, and drinking Ciroc for about an hour. Then Vincent's sister called and invited the girls to her room, to chill with her and her girlfriends.

"Here Vincent, it's your sister," Keisha said, passing Vincent the phone.

"See yall later!" Trina said, getting up to leave with the rest of the girls.

"Talk to you later Poppi," Jessica said to Devin, rubbing his leg on the low as she got up.

"That was my sister. She said the party is already jumping downstairs. She left us some passes at the front with my cousin."

"Damn! It's already 10:30 pm?" Chuck said, hitting the kush stuffed swisher.

"This shit is loud. We need a wet towel to put up under the door!" Devin exclaimed, opening a window.

"I bet I catch me one of these shawtys," Vincent said, headed out the door.

"Not before me," Devin barked.

"Y'all better keep y'all eye on this real mac and peep game," Chuck said, as all four boys got on the elevator, headed down to the party. The hallway entrance to the party was crowded and there was a long line.

Vincent noticed his cousin at the front working the door, so him, Jazz, Chuck, and Devin, walked toward the front, ignoring the long line of people. They could feel the stares and see the questionable looks on the crowd's faces, like who are these fools. The whole crew had that swag and cockiness about themselves. If only people knew it was for a reason; they were the new young crew getting money, and Omaha was about to find out about them. Vincent's cousin noticed them and waived them to the front door.

"What's up Cuz?" Vincent's cousin asked, while staring at the rest of them.

"What's up Kiki?" Vincent spoke back.

"Damn yall fly! Look at y'all, looking like four ballers up in here," Kiki said, impressed with Vincent and his crew. "Here go y'alls bracelets to get back in, if I'm not at the door."

The party was already jumping when they walked in. The dancefloor was packed, and D.J. Mista Soul had the girls droppin it.

"You see all these fine women up in here?" Vincent asked excitedly.

"Look there's Pookie and Preston." Chuck pointed.

Pookie and Preston were two homies from the hood that went to Northwest with Vincent's sister. They both were about eighteen years old and had been hustling for a couple years now. Devin and Vincent use to always watch their stash and their back for the police, and in return they would pay them $20 dollars a piece, but those days were now over.

"Whoa! What's up?" Preston spoke first, noticing his little homies from the hood. "I see y'all looking fresh to death. That's right let 'em know how we do it in Vietnam."

"I see you Devin! You got them new Jordan's too," Pookie said, kicking his feet out to show his.

"Yeah, we killen 'em," Preston said, showing off the pair he had on. Both Preston and Pookie had on different color Polo shirts to match their Jordan's.

"I heard y'all getting that money now. Y'all can come holla whenever. I got a sack for y'all," Preston said.

"Nah, we straight Homie," Vincent and Devin laughed.

They all stood around talking and posin to be chosen, leaning and rocking to the music, as girl after girl of every flavor, fat, skinny, thick, chocolate, white, and redbone, walked by checking them out. Some stopped and talked to Preston and Pookie, while flirting with their eyes at Devin and his crew.

"Hey Devin, look over there," Vincent pointed on the low, at three girls across the room. "She been starin over this way for a minute. That's a bad bitch!" Vincent declared.

"Oh snap! That's old girl from earlier," Devin said, motioning for them to come here.

When the three girls got close, all eyes were on Devin and his crew. Preston and Pookie were surprised.

"What's up Beautiful?" We meet again," Devin greeted Stacy. "You look even better than you did earlier," Devin shot.

"You don't look bad yourself Mr.," Stacy said, checking Devin out from head to toe. She was really impressed with this chocolate stranger that she had met earlier.

"Oh, my bad!" Devin said. "These are my friends." Devin introduced the crew. "This is Stacy, and your name is Pam, right? I don't think I met you. I met Stacy and Pam earlier at the mall."

"So, this is him! My name is Balinda, what's up? We know Pookie and Preston from school, but it's been nice meeting the rest of y'all."

"I'm Devin, that's Jazz, Vincent, and Chuck."

"So y'all having a good time or what?" Preston asked.

"It's cool," Pam answered.

"I didn't know this many people were gonna be here. It's off the chain. The Holiday Inn is a cool spot, you just can't have no drinks in here," Stacy said.

"So, what's up with you Shawty? Ever since I seen you in the mall, I wanted to know all about you, your likes, dislikes, what turns you off, and what turns you on, and keeps you on. I can tell all you need is someone real in your life," Devin shot his game.

"Oh yeah, so when you gonna find out?" Stacy asked, flashing Devin one of the sexiest smiles he had ever seen. "Come on!" Stacy said grabbing Devin's hands, leading him into the middle of the crowd, on the dance floor.

Devin didn't like to dance, but he felt good next to Stacy's soft body, as they grooved to Keisha Cole, whispering in each other's ear with their hands gliding, exploring one another's body. Stacy was impressed and turned on by Devin's hard conditioned body. For some reason she liked being in his arms, while he sang the words to Keisha Cole's song in her ear and his hands played along all the rights spots on her body. She grinded the only spot that wasn't being touched up against Devin's bulge in his pants, and instantly caught fire between her legs. They both were lost in daydreams, when they were interrupted by Balinda.

"Hey Stacy! Me and Pam are about to go to the car."

"Ok! Here I come," Stacy said, in an agitated tone.

"Y'all about to go?" Devin asked.

"No, we just going to the car for a minute, to finish our drinks. I'll be back," Stacy said walking off, throwing her nice ass like a model.

"Damn! She must know I'm looking!" Devin stared, then walked back over to his crew.

"I don't know how you got on shawty, but everybody at Central wanna hit that," Pookie said.

"Fuck Central! Everybody at Northwest wanna hit that too, fool," said Preston.

"She don't go to school with y'all? Devin asked

"No! We go to school with Pam! Those are her friends. Pam is a cheerleader for Northwest, and they cheer for Central."

"Balinda is a freak, we both done hit that before," Pookie smiled, weakly. "What's up with that chick Pam?"

"I don't know. I just met them at the mall today," Devin responded.

"Look!" Jazz pointed to Jessica, Gina, Keisha, and Trina, all dancing together.

"Damn! Who's that redbone?" Pookie asked.

"Her name is Gina! That's my snotty ass homegirl," Chuck said, watching the crew of girls get low.

Bzzz! Bzzz!

"Hello!" Devin yelled into his phone, hard to hear because of the music.

"What's up Homie. I need you," Tina yelled back.

"I can't hear you. I'm gonna call you right back," Devin yelled before hanging up. "I need to make a move real quick and get this money. I'll be back."

"Let that shit wait until tomorrow," Jazz said.

"M.O.B.!" Devin said, giving everybody a pound before he left.

Chapter 28

On Devin's way out the door, he ran into Stacy, Pam, and Balinda coming back in with three dudes he didn't recognize. So, he just made eye contact with Stacy as they were passing each other, and didn't speak.

"Where you going Devin?" He heard Stacy ask, coming up from behind him. "I know you seen me. Why you didn't say nothing?"

"I didn't know if one of them dudes was your man or what, and I didn't want to put you on blast. I gotta make a quick run to the hood. I'm coming back," Devin said, turning to walk away.

"I don't' have a man, Devin. Can I go with you? Let me tell my homegirls I'm leaving with you, I'll be back," Stacy said, not waiting for Devin to give her a yes or no answer.

"Hurry up! I'll pick you up in the front," Devin said.

"Ok! Here I come," Stacy said, hurrying inside.

By the time Devin made it to the car and drove back around front, Stacy was already out there waiting." Devin pulled up next to her and lowered the tinted window. "Come on!" Devin called out to Stacy to get in.

"Nice car," Stacy said, climbing in.

Devin drove off without saying a word, taking the interstate from 72nd Street, back to North Omaha.

"I know you not trippin about them dudes you seen me with. They ain't nobody to me. We were just firing up with them outside, since they had a little marijuana." Stacy tried to explain, thinking that was the reason Devin was so quiet.

"I'm not thinking about that. You are not my woman, I can't trip on you Shawty," Devin said, dialing Tina's number into his phone, then pressing the send button. Devin listened, as Tina's phone rang several times before she answered.

"Hello!"

"What's up Homegirl?"

"I need to see you!"

"Meet me at the spot. I'm on my way to the hood now," Devin said, before hanging up. "Can you roll?" Devin asked, reaching into his glove box to get the bag of kush.

"Yeah!"

Devin grabbed a cigarillo, the thrifty nickel newspaper to roll it on, a couple of buds of the loud to roll up, and gave it to Stacy.

"This that good dro," Stacy said, smiling as she finished rolling the cigarillo. "Them dudes you seen us with had that reggie."

"That's that good kush, we only smoke that strong."

"So, what's up with you Devin? Why yo fine chocolate self ain't wit your girl?"

"I don't have a girl. I'm a hustla baby. I haven't had time to really get to chill with a female."

"Like the way we are?" Stacy asked, as she lit the marijuana, coughing on her first puff.

"I guess, yeah like this." Devin just shrugged it off as nothing, then grabbed the swisher being passed to him. "Don't get me wrong, I'm not gay or nothing. I would love to have a beautiful girl like you around to chill with, but I ain't got time for that. I'm trying to get this money right now, and that's all that's on my mind. You feel me?"

"Yeah, I feel you, but I don't want all your time Devin, just a little bit," Stacy said, sliding closer up under Devin.

Devin took a long drag on the cigarillo. He inhaled then exhaled, blowing out a big cloud of smoke. The kush mixed with R. Kelly's Greatest Hits, had started to take affect on both of them.

"I like you Devin. The way you walk, the way you talk, and the way you carry yourself is so different from what I am use to," Stacy said, in a sensuous tone, as her hands rubbed up and down Devin's arm. She reclined back into her seat, enjoying the music and floating off the kush.

They rode in silence and stared at each other on the low, both trying to hide their lustful gazes.

"You like what you see?" Stacy asked, noticing Devin's eyes locking back and forth from the highway to between her legs.

"You have some pretty legs," Devin responded, reaching over and rubbing his hands up and down the insides of her legs, from her knee to her panties.

Stacy passed the last of the marijuana roach to Devin, then spread her legs as wide as she could get them in the front seat of the Maxima, all you could see was honey brown legs and red panties. Devin took one last puff of the cigarillo, thumped it out the window, then returned his hands between Stacy's legs. Stacy was loving the soft touch of Devin's hands rubbing up and down the sensitive part of her inner leg. She let out a soft sexy moan and closed her eyes, as Devin's hand made its way inside her moist panties. Devin rubbed his hand up and down the soft bareness of her pussy, pressing down across her clit on every stroke, letting one finger then two, slide inside her. She felt so hot and sticky inside, as Devin worked his fingers. Stacy started to arch her back and pelvis out of the seat, fucking

Devin's fingers to the rhythm. All you could hear was moans, R. Kelly, and the wet wet sound from Stacy's jewel box.

Ssss…ooohhh…pleeaasse don't stop I…I…I'm cuming." Stacy screamed, fucking Devin's fingers uncontrollably, as they pulled up in the projects and parked in the space behind the trap house. Stacy stared curiously at the rows and rows of brick buildings, consisting of hundreds of individual apartments. The projects looked like a world of its own at night.

"Where we at?" Stacy turned in her seat, with that lustful look in her eyes.

"We are in my hood Shawty. Everything's cool back here," Devin said, with sex on his mind, until he saw Tina's car pulling up.

"Hold on for a minute Shawty, I'll be right back," Devin said, getting out of the car.

"What's up D?" Tina said, walking up to meet Devin.

"Same shit Homie," Devin said, as the backdoor opened, just when they were about to walk up on the porch.

"What's up y'all?" Jamarl said, unlocking the screen door.

"What you trying to get up on Homegirl?" Devin asked, when they walked into the kitchen and closed the door.

"Let me get an ounce," Tina said, giving Devin the stack of bills.

"Hold on." Devin ran up to his room, grabbed the ounce, ran back downstairs, handed the ounce to Tina, then told Jamarl he was leaving.

On the way back to the party, Stacy was all over Devin, kissing his neck, ears, and chest, as her hands massaged his lap.

"Why you doing me like this? You got me going crazy in my shorts," Devin said, breathing into Stacy's ear as he drove.

"Let him out then." Stacy smiled while unbuckling Devin's belt and unzipping his pants.

Devin's hard on popped out to full attention, with Stacy not having to use her hands to free it from his boxers. Devin moved his seat back and adjusted the steering wheel giving Stacy more room, as he drove on the highway. Stacy lifted Devin's shirt with one hand, kissing him all over, leaving shivering wet trails from his chest down to his tight abs.

"Uh...mmm," Devin let out moans of pleasure as Stacy's cold hands and wet mouth made its way around the head of his dick. "Yeah, like that Baby," Devin groaned and squirmed back into his seat as Stacy's tongue swirled around the tip, then down his pole.

Bzzz! Bzzz! Devin's phone vibrated in his shorts.

"Awwww shit!!!"

"Hhellloo!" Devin answered his phone in ecstasy.

"Where you at Homie?" Jessica's asking about you!" Vincent noticed the pause and heavy breathing in Devin's voice.

"Uhmmm..., huh? Say that again Vinc..." Devin had to ask, because Stacy's bomb head game had him distracted.

"I said where you at?" Vincent reiterated.

"I'm pulling up now," Devin said, getting off the 72nd Street exit. Devin hung up the phone, then looked down and watched as his dick disappeared and reappeared at the expense of Stacy's wet mouth. He played in the hair on top of her head with his right hand, grabbing a handful, helping her up and down, trying his best not to cum, as she pleased him. "We here!" Devin exclaimed, putting the car in park in the back of the parking lot. All you could hear was the slurping sounds from Stacy's wet mouth, going up and down on Devin's pole. "Uhhh...shit...,"

Devin said, legs shaking, as he pumped up from his seat into Stacy's mouth, who had turned the pace up and took Devin deeper into her mouth and throat. "Oooh shit." Devin shook, feeling the sparks from his toes to his nut sack. It was like Stacy could feel the same thing as she took Devin all the way into her mouth working her tongue around at the same time. "Ahhhhh...shiiittt IIImmm cummmiiinnnggg." Devin erupted like a volcano down Stacy's throat, and she tried to swallow every drop. Devin pumped out of the seat uncontrollably, until the last piece of energy left his body. He wiped the sweat off his forehead, then pulled his pants up.

"Damn! Look what you did to my hair." Stacy said, looking in the mirror trying to get herself together. "I can't go back in there like this, take me to my car."

Devin pulled up to the same Chrysler 300 he had seen Stacy getting into at the mall. "Call me!" Devin said, as Stacy climbed out of the Maxima.

"I'm gonna call you when I drop my homegirls off, aight! Stacy smiled.

"Talk to you later Shawty," Devin said, waiting for Stacy to get in her car, before he pulled around to the front.

Chapter 29

The party was just about over when Devin got back inside. The first people he saw when he walked through the door were Pookie, Chuck, Pam, and Balinda.

"What's up Homie?" Vincent and them are over there," Chuck pointed. "I'm about to go back to the hood. Ima ride with Pookie."

"Where's my homegirl at?" Belinda asked, in a weary tone.

"She's outside waiting for y'all in her car," Devin said, smiling.

"Damn you smiling and walking in here on your toes and shit, old girl must got some bomb! I know you took care of your business."

"Yeah, the money and the honey," Devin said, and they all started laughing and giving pounds.

"That's what I'm talking about. Give me my money fool!" Chuck said, jumping up and down laughing, holding his hands out to get paid from Pookie. "Yo, I bet those fools you was gonna knock shawty. Him and Preston was doubting our game, and he gonna owe me another $50 bucks because her homegirl Pam is all on my line Homie. I told them fools to watch out for us. We dem new boys in the hood!" Chuck exclaimed, giving Devin a pound.

"Whateva fool," Pookie said, paying off his bet he lost to Chuck. "You ready to bounce?"

"We out D. I'll holla at cha tomorrow. I can't let Jamarl stay in the trap all night by himself," Chuck said, leaving out the door with Pookie.

Devin walked through the crowd swagging to the music, until he spotted his crew sitting at the table by the D.J. booth.

"What's up? Y'all look tired," Devin said, to Vincent and Jazz.

"We are fucked up, been drinking some mixed shit with my sister and her friends," Vincent said.

"Where they at?" Devin asked.

"There they go!" Jazz pointed to the dance floor.

When Devin turned and looked, he noticed Jessica staring at him, so he waved. Jessica smiled and waved back, while her and the rest of the girls moved their bodies like a snake to the R. Kelly song that was blastin through the speakers.

"I don't see Gina!" Devin said.

"I think she left with Preston," Vincent said, smiling.

"Hey! We are about to go to my room; this is the last song anyway. What's up D? I was wondering what happened to you?" Vincent's sister said, as they all headed upstairs to her room.

The room was crowded and loud as they played a drinking trivia game, boys against girls. Vincent's sister and his cousin both had their boyfriends, Famo and John-John with them. They were crips, but you could tell they were all about their money. The game was fun until both teams were drunk, and they all settled down to watch a scary movie DVD that Johnetta put in. Everyone claimed different areas in the dark room to cuddle. It was about 2:30 in the morning, when Devin and Jessica decided to creep up to their room.

It seemed like forever before the elevator finally came down, and they got inside. Devin turned to Jessica, pulled her to him, and gave her a huge wet kiss. Jessica had been teasing Devin in Johnetta's room, and because of that, ever since they got into the elevator, Devin's dick was fat and hard. Devin could feel Jessica's nipples stiffening when he grabbed a handful, pinching them between his thumb and fore finger, when they kissed, Jessica moaned and grabbed for Devin's pants, unbuckling his belt and zipper, only to be stopped by a pair of boxers.

"Hold up," Devin huffed, after he broke his lips free from hers, feeling the elevator stopping at their floor. "We gonna get caught fucking in this elevator, if you don't come on!" Devin said, as the elevator door opened.

Jessica smiled the sexiest come fuck me smile Devin had ever seen. They both rushed out of the elevator into the room. As soon as they were in the room, Devin pulled Jessica to him, lifted her shirt up over her head, and wrapped his mouth and lips around her swollen brown nipples, sucking the soft meaty tissue almost completely. They stumbled around, falling against the wall in a dizzy display of Ciroc, kush, and sexual arousal. Devin's hands were all over Jessica, and she was still tugging at his pants insisting that they come off.

"Come on Devin, get rid of these," Jessica moaned between breaths. "I want to see it."

Devin stood on the side of the bed and slid off his shorts, then his boxers. His dick stood proudly for her. Jessica's jaw dropped. Devin could tell she was impressed with what he was working with.

"Get undressed," Devin said.

Jessica unzipped her Roca Wear skirt and kicked it off along with her shoes, showing Devin her perfect little bare feet, with pink painted toenails. Her panties were white cotton. Devin sat down on the bed and pulled Jessica by her hips to him. He was face to pussy. She smelled of perfume, a mixture of "Halle" a fragrance by Halle Berry and her own scent. Inch by inch of Jessica's bald pussy was revealed to Devin, as he pulled her panties down over her flawless butt cheeks. When Devin got them down to her knees, she kicked them off, then climbed into the bed beside Devin.

Devin laid on top of Jessica with half his body on the bed. He thrusted his fingers slowly into the wet puddle of her pussy. Devin met little resistance. Jessica's pussy was tight. Devin sucked on her pointy nipples and played in her juice box until it was dripping, then he grabbed a rubber out of his jeans pocket and rolled it on. He explored between Jessica's legs. The slippery noises of Devin's sloshing fingers filled the air with Jessica's moans and pleas for more. She was soaked and Devin was ready to do the nasty. Devin climbed on top of Jessica and kissed her some more, as he used his legs to push hers apart. She opened them, so that one foot was on the bed and the other one on the wall. Devin aimed his dickhead without the aid of his hands and found her wet tight spot, with a few testing jabs, as he grabbed her hips and held her tight, bracing her, plunging in only a few inches.

Jessica's eyes were open wide and staring right into Devin's. Her lips were parted, and her breath was coming in short sharp gasps. "Give it to me Poppi!" Jessica whispered.

Devin forced himself to push harder, as if it was like separating a vice, plunging into Jessica's firm wet pussy walls. She was getting wetter, and Devin was going deeper. He was sweating from the effort, but couldn't let up. Devin fucked Jessica wildly. All you could hear were groans, the wet wet sounds from her sex, and their bodies slapping together.

Long stroke! Short stroke! Devin was assaulting Jessica's love box, trying to clear his mind from the murder he had committed earlier. He was beating Jessica's pussy up, and she loved it. Her eyes rolled to the back of her head and her orgasm thundered through her whole body. Jessica gripped and dug her nails into Devin's ass making him slam deeper into her vibrating pussy. It was more than Devin could take. He gave her a few more thrusts and at the same time, told her he was coming. They were both warn out, but not completely. They rolled up, smoked, then fucked once more that night, doggy style, before they fell asleep.

∞ ∞ ∞ ∞ ∞ ∞ ∞ ∞ ∞ ∞

Devin woke up early. The sun was shining bright and the rays spread across the dark room, through the open parts of the curtain onto Jessica's naked body, as she lay sound asleep next to Devin.

"I got so much shit to do today," Devin said under his breath, not wanting to wake Jessica. He raised the covers and stared at the rest of Jessica's beautiful flawless naked body, before getting out of bed and into the shower. When Devin was finished showering, Jessica was already dressed sitting on the bed.

"What's up Poppi? You're up early, are you hungry?"

"Yeah, a little!"

"I'm about to run downstairs to get me something. What do you want?" Jessica asked.

"Get me some waffles, eggs scrambled with cheese, orange juice, and some sausage or bacon."

"I thought you said you was a little hungry," Jessica said laughing, on her way out the door.

While Jessica was gone, Devin finished getting dressed then fired up the half cigarillo kush that was left from last night.

Knock! Knock!

"Why didn't you take the key?" Devin asked, getting up to open the door, for who he thought was Jessica knocking.

"Yo, what up D? Damn it smells like sex and kush incense in here," Vincent said, walking in laughing.

"What cha think I got the room for, to sleep fool? Jessica got that wet wet. All we did was smoke and fuck all night."

"Where she at?" Vincent asked, staring around as if he was looking for Jessica.

"She went downstairs to get us some breakfast. What you doing up so early?"

"Trina gotta get her mom's car back before she notices that it's missing, so I came to tell Jessica to hurry up. Why y'all up so early?"

"I told you they are delivering the furniture to the spot this morning. I have to be there with the receipt and purchase order. Then I gotta go holla at Taco, because I don't have much work left. How you living?" Devin asked.

"I only got a couple ounces left. I was gonna piece for piece 'em out. Yo you didn't see the news?" Vincent answered his own question, noticing Devin didn't have the TV on.

Knock! Knock! There was a knock at the door.

"No why? What's up?" Devin asked Vincent, who was opening the door.

"What's up Vincent?" Said Jessica, walking into the room with a tray of food, and a newspaper.

"What's up Shawty?"

"Poppi! The newspaper got your homeboy on the front page wanted for murder."

"That's what I was about to tell you," Vincent responded.

Jessica gave Devin his breakfast and the newspaper. "I gotta go Poppi, Trina is outside waiting on me. I will call you later," Jessica said, grabbing the rest of her things, before heading out the door.

Devin put his breakfast down and started reading the newspaper.

Man Slain During Robbery

North Omaha Police were searching Friday for the gunman responsible for the city's 25th homicide of the year. Police have not retrieved a weapon, but said the victim, twenty-six-year-old James McCoy, was shot to death in a robbery. Cops were called to the scene of a reported homicide about 4:30 pm Friday at 23rd and Paul Street, in the Logan Fontenelle Housing Projects. A man described by witnesses as a long-time friend of the McCoy's, knocked on his door about 2:35 pm, in an attempt to rob him. When McCoy came to the door, the suspect shot him on the porch, with a 38-caliber revolver. After taking a slug to the head, McCoy geeked off an adrenaline rush, jumped off the porch and ran down the street about a block, where he collapsed and died.

Police identified twenty-four-year-old Robert Prater as a person of interest in the case, and are searching for him. He is considered to be armed and dangerous. Anyone with information is asked to call the Omaha Police department at 402-455-6700.

"Damn! That shit is crazy. I seen that fool RIP yesterday at Nebraska Furniture Mart. He asked me for some dope, but the fool was looking all crazy with his hands in his pockets, high beams looking around like he was nervous. I told that fool ain't nothin poppin, to catch me in the hood. I can't believe that fool killed J. MC!" Devin said, shaking his head in disbelief.

"Yeah, you might have gotten lucky. He could have smoked you," Vincent said, in a serious tone.

"Have you seen Jazz? I'm about to ride out."

"Yeah! Him and Keisha stayed with us last night. They slept in the other bed. He was still sleep when I left. I got some wild shit to tell you about last night. I'll catch you at the spot later, so we can talk. Don't trip, I will take Jazz home," Vincent said, giving Devin a pound, as they walked into the hall.

Chapter 30

It only took the movers and their electronics geek squad about two hours to move all the furniture into the house, set up the flat screen TV's on the walls with the theater surround sound, and put both beds and the living room tables up. Jackie had paid extra for delivery and assembly. After the movers had left, Devin and Chuck sat on the couch, starry-eyed at the way their trap spot looked, now with the furniture.

Devin felt proud of himself and the direction he was taking himself and his crew, which was to the top. All the players, hustlers, fiends, women, and gangsters would respect their mind and grind.

"We need to call Tina and let her know to keep the Cox Cable turned on over here in her name," Chuck said relaxing back into the soft leather sofa, watching ESPN on a fifty-inch flat screen TV, mounted on the living room wall.

"Yeah, make sure you do that. Between you and Jamarl, give her enough money to pay six months' rent, the light bill, and the cable up front. Me and Vincent took care of the furniture and stuff. We all gotta do our part, this is our spot! Me, you, Vincent, and Jamarl's. Our shit is gonna stay clean, and the bills gonna stay paid. This is how we livin Homie!"

Bzzz! Bzzz!

"No doubt!" Chuck said to Devin, who was answering his phone.

"Ok! MTV cribs in the hood," Jamarl shouted, walking into the living room from the back. "This is serious! Look at this shit!" Jamarl looked around in amazement. "Look like somebody won the lottery in this bitch. Man, this is fly," Jamarl said, smiling ear to ear.

"Yeah! I'm glad they came early. You should have seen how the people that was up this morning was looking when they was moving this stuff in here. Somebody gone have to be here all the time," Chuck said.

"What's up Jamarl? You like?" Devin asked, getting off the phone.

"Hell yeah! I didn't know you had it like this. You doing big things Homie."

"No! We doing big things! We got it like this! This is our spot Homie! Me, you, Vincent, and Chuck, so make sure you save some of that money you made last night for the bills." Devin smiled weakly.

"Speaking of last night D, it was crazy. Motha fuckas came through all night, pimps, hos, and fiends; everybody. At about 3:00 this morning the kitchen was full of motha fuckas lined up to spend money from all over town. Tell 'em Chuck," Jamarl boasted.

"Yeah, it was off the chain D. I know I made $500 dollars from the time I got here. At about 1:30 this morning till now, every time I thought I was gonna fall asleep, somebody knocked on the door to get served, and it's still rolling," Chuck smiled, hearing a knock at the backdoor.

"Every day I'm hustlin, hustlin," Jamarl sang, going into the kitchen to answer the door.

"This is what I'm talking about. Hell yeah! You the man Homie," Vincent's voice reflected loudly in Devin's direction, as he jumped around excited, like a kid on Christmas, when he walked in the front door and noticed all the new stuff. "Damn! I didn't know you had put it down like this," Vincent said, looking around.

"I ain't fakin Homie," Devin shrugged everything off as nothing. "V, check this out," said Devin, running up the stairs. "Go check your room out," Devin said, unlocking his own room door, then jumping on his new bed happily. Devin grabbed the remote to his new TV and stereo and blasted his "Dirty Chuck" CD.

"Uh-huh…uh-huh…" Vincent whooped and yelled with extreme excitement from the other bedroom. "This shit is gangsta Homie," Vincent said, coming into Devin's room. How you pull this off?" Vincent asked with admiration, giving Devin his half of the money on the furniture and stuff.

"Money," Devin whooped throwing the money in the air, making it rain bills down on them. "That's how! It's our time to shine Homie."

"Oh yeah, I almost forgot, I dropped Jazz off at the Boys Club. You know we got an all-team tryout today? It's a tournament this week. The tryouts start at 11:00 am, its 10:45 am now, you going?"

"Yeah, I'm going. What about you?"

"I gotta get this money first, because I got some people waiting for me. Tell Coach Kenny I'm gonna be a little late."

"Fo sho," Devin said, stuffing all the money from his pockets and off the floor from when he made it rain, into his backpack with the rest of his money, before locking his door and running downstairs. Holla at y'all later." Devin threw Jamarl the crack he had left in his backpack. "I'll get these chips from you later. I gotta hurry up and get to the house so I can change," Devin said headed into the kitchen, because he had parked Jackie's Maxima in the back.

When Devin got home his mom was still in the bed sleep with her company, so he crept by her room not wanting to wake her. He stashed his money away, grabbed some gym shorts and shoes, and started to head back out.

"Devin is that you?" His mom called from her room, when he passed back by her door.

"Yes Mom! I forgot something, gotta go love you," Devin stated, in a nervous tone, as he ran down the stairs and out the door.

Chapter 31

"Damn! I got seven missed calls," Devin said looking at his phone, as him and Vincent were leaving tryouts at the Boys Club.

"I got some missed calls too," Vincent said, after turning his phone on.

"I think we have a better team now, what do you think V?" Devin asked as him and Vincent walked down the street, headed to his house.

"I don't see nobody fuckin with us from the Midwest this year. We should have won regionals last year," Vincent said sternly.

"I like them two new white boys from Elkhorn. They are tough."

"6' 8" and 6' 10", plus they play like their black. I ain't never seen white boys hoop like them, except that white boy on that team we played from Florida last year, in the Vegas tournament."

"Remember everybody was calling that fool White Chocolate?"

"Did you see the pass I gave the 6' 10" red head? The one when he dunked on Percy?" Devin asked.

"Yeah, that was nice, but I was droppin that tear drop on they tall asses until coach put them with us," Vincent bragged.

"Me, you, Jazz, and them white boys are gonna be the starters watch and see. You see how we was running shit in the scrimmage. It was like we played together before," Devin said, as they walked in the house and saw his mom in the kitchen cooking.

"Did y'all win?" Devin's mom asked, when she noticed the two sweaty boys come in the door.

"You know it," Devin said.

"Boyyyy, you think you all that," Devin's mom teased like she always did. The truth is, she knew her son was good.

"I know I'm all that," Devin said, going up the stairs laughing.

"Are y'all hungry?" Devin's mom hollered up the stairs behind them.

"No ma'am."

"What? Speak for yourself," Vincent said, shooting a playful jab at Devin.

"You want something?"

"Hell yeah, after all that runnin they had us doing."

"Hold up!" Devin said, running down the stairs to the kitchen. "What cha cooking Mom?" He asked, looking over his mom's shoulder, planting a kiss on her jaw.

"Fried pork chops, fried potatoes, eggs and toast," Devin's mom responded, as she playfully shrugged Devin off her backside.

"Yeah, we want some! I changed my mind. Where did your friend go?" Devin asked, while making him and Vincent fried pork chop sandwiches.

"He went to the store to get some milk and orange juice. Did you wash your hands?"

"Yes Mom," Devin replied, with a mouthful of food and two porkchop sandwiches, headed back upstairs.

"Yo phone was vibrating like crazy. I started to answer it, but then mine started going off too," Vincent said, as he laid across Devin's bed, talking on the phone.

"Get yo sweaty ass out my bed!" Devin said, pushing send on his last missed call.

"What's up D?" The familiar voice said on the phone.

"What's up Taco?" Devin asked, with excitement.

"I've been trying to get in contact with you since we got here. What's up?" Taco stated, in a serious tone.

"We just got out of basketball practice, my bad Big Homie. Where you at?"

"At the house on Spaulding Street. I'll be there in about ten minutes," Devin said, before hanging up. "That was Taco, they're back. You going with me to take care of this business?"

"Nah, I gotta take care of some shit in the hood. Just holla at me when you get back," Vincent said, getting off the bed, headed to the bathroom.

"Make sure you wash your hands fool!" Devin joked.

Devin was sitting on the bed counting money when Vincent came back in the room rubbing his stomach.

"That's how you gonna do it V? Come over my house and blow it up?" Devin asked, holding his nose with a frown.

"My bad Homie. I had to use it bad."

I'm not trippin Homie. I was just jokin with you, better out than in," Devin said, headed downstairs to let Vincent out. "Take this with you." Devin handed Vincent one of the sandwiches.

Chapter 32

It took Devin about thirty minutes to count and rubber band seven $5,000 dollar bundles from his stash spots. He stood at the front of his bed glowing with happiness at the 35,000 dollars that laid on his bed. Devin was stunned he made more money hustling for one month, than he had ever seen put together in his young life. After paying Taco his money for the half brick, he would still have twenty-six thousand dollars. That alone had Devin dumbfounded, but eager to hustle harder. *Y'all think y'all getting money.* He thought to himself about some of his older homies and hustlers that he's known from around the area. "Watch this true hustler fo real ask Puff Daddy," Devin sang Biggie's verse, placing the money and the two bricks of dope into his backpack, and headed out.

"Mom I'm about to go outside," Devin said, stopping at his mom's bedroom door that was now closed.

"Don't forget your key," his mom barked, as he was headed out the door.

Devin ran around the block, popped the trunk with the remote, then placed the backpack in it. Thinking about not hearing from Jackie or Crisi yet, Devin decided to call them. He vibed out to Jeezy, as Jackie's phone rang several times.

"Hello!" Jackie's sexy soft voice answered.

"What's up Shawty? Why y'all haven't called?"

"Oh, my baby misses us already," Jackie said playfully.

"I was just trying to make sure y'all was ok. I didn't say nothing about missing y'all," Devin stated, in a sarcastic tone.

"Whateva! We had a change of plans. We are in Minnesota and should be back tomorrow night. What are you doing?"

"Just came from basketball practice, on my way to take care of some business," Devin stated, headed down 30th Street, about to take a right on Spaulding, when he noticed some of his older homies from the hood, standing in the lot between Kelly's detail carwash and the Spaulding Bar. They were talking to a group of girls, when Devin pulled in the lot and parked behind them.

"I was just checking up on y'all. I'll talk to you later gotta go, be safe," Devin said, getting out the car.

"We will call you later Boo. You be careful," Jackie said, before hanging up the phone.

All eyes were on Devin, as he exited the Maxima. "What's up y'all?" Devin said to his homies who appeared to be a little startled, until they noticed that it was Devin getting out of the car.

"It ain't nobody but the little homie D," Preston said to Herb.

"What's up Little Homie?" Preston and Herb greeted Devin, taking their hands from under their shirts, where nine times out of ten, they had their guns.

"I heard you getting the money now relative," Herb said. Herb was Devin's first cousin. Devin's mom and Herb's mom were sisters. Herb was six years older than Devin, and already had a reputation in the street for getting money and poppin that pistol.

"Runs in the family!" Devin smiled weakly, not knowing how his cousin would react to his admission of being in the game.

"Fo sho! Ima holla at cha later to see what's good," Herb said, before turning his attention back to the crowd of girls.

"What's up D?" Milo asked, walking over giving Devin a pound. Milo was one of the O.G.'s from the hood, who had just gotten out of the pen. He was ripped with muscles everywhere. Devin could tell most of the girls in the crowd were attracted to him, from the way they stared at him, in his wife beater.

"Did you hit that last night? I heard y'all crept off," Preston asked.

"I heard you crept off too," Devin responded, deciding not to answer Preston's question because he had already caught a couple of the girls in the crowd eyeballing him on the low.

"Kelly, this my little homie D. He needs his whip cleaned. Take care of him for me," Milo said before reaching inside, turning the car off.

"We were closing up after we finished Herb's car! He gave me $50 bucks or we would have been closed after we cleaned yours."

"Hook me up O.G.," Devin said passing Kelly a $50 dollar bill.

"That's what I like to see! Money talks, where's your car?" Kelly asked, placing the money in his pocket.

"The Maxima right there!" Devin pointed.

"Let me get the keys. I will have it finished in about thirty minutes," Kelly said, before walking off to pull the Maxima inside the shop.

"I told you Lil Homie, he's good people. He's gonna get you right," Milo said, getting inside his clean Chevy and dropping the top.

The 1966 Chevy was the cleanest car Devin had ever seen, and when Milo dropped the top and rolled the windows down, the crocodile blue leather seats, were exposed.

"Hold up, let me grab something out of my trunk," Devin yelled to Kelly, who was about to pull the Maxima inside the shop. Devin ran over, grabbed his backpack, and got into the clean Chevy with Milo, who had motioned for him to get in.

"We about to hit the strip," Milo said to Devin, when he noticed them backing Herb's clean Chevy out. "Yo Herb your shit it done. Come on fool," Milo yelled, sitting on twenty-six-inch Asantis, that belonged to his cousin Herb.

Ba bump! Ba bump bump! The two fifteen-inch Sound Stream subwoofers in the custom fiberglass enclosure, came to life with "Yo Gotti" pounding out, as the 454-fuel inducted crate motor came roaring to life when Milo started the engine.

"Yo, I would love to ride with y'all but I gotta handle this business," Devin said getting out of the car even though he really wanted to ride out with them. He knew he had business to take care of.

"I'll bring you back in a minute Homie, come on! The strip is packed with girls everywhere fool."

"I'll holla at y'all later Big Homie. Y'all already right, I'm trying to get right!" Devin said, as he slung the backpack over his shoulders and headed out the back of the lot, across the field to Taco's spot. Devin could hear the Chevy's behind him growl and beat down 30th Street, as he walked on the porch and rang the doorbell.

Chapter 33

"Who is it?" The unfamiliar voice behind the door asked in an authoritative tone.

"Lil D."

The door opened with some dude Devin had never seen before, mugging him up and down. Devin gave the dude who was probably about nineteen or twenty the same ice grill up and down, before asking for Taco.

"Taco! Somebody named Lil D is at the door for you," The stranger turned and yelled.

Devin didn't like being stopped at the door by the shirtless stranger in the baggy black Polo shorts, and black high-top Prada tennis shoes, and he really didn't like how the stranger was mugging him.

"Let 'em in fool and close the door. You letting all them flies in. That's my little homie I was telling y'all about," Taco yelled from the living room.

Devin brushed past the dude at the door without waiting for him to turn around and say anything.

"What's up Lil D? Come on back here," Taco said, as he raised up off the couch in the living room, walking toward the kitchen.

"What's up Big Homie?" Devin said to Taco, noticing the three new faces in the living room full of loud smoke.

"Ain't nothin Little Homie. I'm just trying to get this money together before we bounce."

"Before you bounce?" Devin asked, his voice urgent.

"We are gonna drive out to Denver tonight."

"Damn Big Homie I need you. Here go your money for the half a brick...But I'm ready for the whole thing. I know I can handle a whole key, what's up? I got the money," Devin said, disappointed that Taco was leaving.

"You already finished with that half a brick you got from me? And you got the money to buy a whole brick?" Taco asked, impressed with his little young potna's hustle.

Devin had only been in the game a month, and already he was trying to buy his own bird. What really impressed Taco, was that Devin reminded him so much of himself. Taco had been in the game since he was fourteen, and finally now that he was in his late twenties, did he have millions of dollars, houses, whips, women, and everything he wanted he could buy, all because his dad had schooled him to the game before he died at an early age, leaving Taco with one hundred bricks of his own. Taco had never looked back. He elevated his hustle around the world, but never had he come across a kid with the hustle and grind like young Devin. He could see it in Devin's eyes, as if he was looking in the mirror at himself.

"Don't get me wrong Little Homie. I like you Devin, but you see everybody in this house, we are like a family. We have been getting money together for a long time, because we trust each other and have loyalty to each other. No snitches, no fighting over bitches, no disrespect in this game. You gotta have some kind of honor and character about yourself. I see that your hustle is all the way turned up, but what's up with your heart? Can you handle pressure?"

"I ain't no punk or rat! Its T.Y.C. where I am from, 'Take Your Charge' and I am ready to get respect in the hood for holdin mine. I'm good from the shoulders and I will pop that gun Big Homie."

All Taco could do was shake his head. He knew that Devin had everything it took to be successful in this game, and what he didn't know already, Taco would teach him.

"Lil D, your grind and your heart is way past your age, but I'm gonna take you to the next level with this game, show you how to really flip this money instead of fuckin it off on bullshit. Don't get me wrong, we gotta stay fresh, but flip that money first, then you can do what 'cha want and still have money on deck. "You see everybody in that room?" Taco gestured with his head. "They are all rich and still money hungry. We are getting money all around the world, but I am tired Little Homie. I don't want to come out here anymore. I just want to sit at home and count money and smoke on this good Cali bud," Taco said, as he puffed on the blunt that one of his friends passed him.

"I put that on everything I love Big Homie, I am ready. You can put me in the game, and you don't have to play out here no more. I can handle everything, just lace me one time to what needs to be done and I will handle it. I got more money than I have ever seen in my life because of you Big Homie, but just like y'all, I am still money hungry," Devin said, before taking a long puff from the blunt Taco passed him.

Taco contemplated on his next move, as he stared at Devin puffing on the blunt. "Don't let me down," Taco said, mind made up about adding Devin to the family.

"I won't Big Homie. Ima grind harder." Devin said excited.

"So how was practice? I didn't know you hooped, are you any good? Did you make the team?" Taco asked changing the subject, and grabbing the blunt back from Devin.

"Practice was cool, we got some new players, so we are better than we were last year. I am like that, Big Homie! I always make the AAU team. All the coaches from the Nebraska area want me and Vincent to play for their teams, but we stay loyal to Coach Kenny because just like us, most of the people on his team come from the hood, broken homes and no dads. I had never flown on a plane, stayed at a hotel, or dined at a restaurant, until I started playing for Coach Kenny. He checks up on us in the hood and at school to make sure we are straight, and our grades are good. So, I always turn those rich white coaches down when they try to recruit me to play for their AAU teams. Don't get me wrong the free shoes and stuff they offer gets tempting, but I always stay loyal to Coach Kenny's team."

"I like that Little Homie, trust and loyalty is gonna help you get rich, and me a little richer," Taco said laughing. "I'm gonna have to come check out some of your games. Oh yeah, I almost forgot, here you go," Taco said, handing Devin a big suitcase.

"What's this?" Devin asked, looking at the suitcase curiously.

"Some clothes and a couple pairs of shoes. I got a little carried away trying to get some gear for you. I didn't know what you liked, but I gotcha some clothes. I had so many bags of clothes and shit I had to get a suitcase to bring on the plane."

"How much I owe you?" Devin said, pulling out a larger rubber banded roll of money.

"Ok I see you, but it's a gift Little Homie, you don't owe me nothing. You family now. Everybody around me stays fresh," Taco said, looking around at everybody in the room. "That's how we do."

"Good looking out Big Homie, but what I really need is to buy one of these birds," Devin said, placing his hands-on top of the backpack.

"Damn, I forgot all about this shit!" Taco said, unzipping the bag and pulling out the two birds of dope.

"I told you I would hold you down Big Homie. I had to get off the 4-5 because it got dirty. A fool got down wrong, and I had to use it. Just let me know how much I owe you?"

"Don't trip about that gun. Just make sure you get rid of it and stay out of trouble. You can't make no money at war, but if you need another strap, I got one; better safe than sorry."

"I feel you! It was something that had to be done, if I'm gonna be out here getting money."

"Speaking of money, here's what I'm gonna do Lil D! You can get this one for seventeen and I will front you this other one for twenty," Taco said, pushing the two kilos of dope across the table to Devin.

"What if I pay for 'em both today? How much you gonna charge me?"

"B-both of 'em?" Taco stuttered, surprised. "Let me see!" Taco paused to think about the question young Devin had surprised him with. "Fuck it, give me $30,000 dollars Lil Homie. Can you get that much money together today before we leave?" Taco asked, doubtful.

"No doubt, I'll be back in about an hour with the money," Devin said, getting up to leave. He was so happy about what was getting ready to happen.

"Don't forget your stuff," Taco said, placing the two keys of dope into the suitcase with Devin's clothes, before handing Devin the suitcase.

"I was gonna get it when I came back with the money."

"Trust and loyalty Lil Homie. I will be here when you get back, but you can take your stuff with you."

"Ok but let me run across the street and get my car from the detail shop first. I don't want to get bumped by the police because they think I ran away from home, walking down the street with this suitcase."

"What? What kind of whip you got Little Homie?" Taco asked surprised.

"A little clean Maxima. It's not mine, it's my girl's," Devin said headed out the door to pick up his car from Kelly's.

Young Money
Volume 2 Crumbs to Bricks

Coming Soon!!!!!

Please do a book review on Amazon.com and be sure to tell your friends about the "Young Money" series.

Thank you very much!

Darius Christian

About the Author, Darius Christian:

Darius Christian is an incredible author from Omaha, Nebraska who writes thought provoking books about life and love; raising the bar, creating new levels of artistic works, that are helping to expand the literary community.

He was born in Fort Smith, Arkansas to a single mother, Sandra Christian, in 1969. He was raised by his mom, grandmother, grandfather, and aunties in the 39th unit of The Elm Grove Projects in Fort Smith, Arkansas, and raised in the bottoms of North Omaha, Nebraska

Darius is a Certified Personal Trainer, HVAC Universal Technician, Troubled Youth Counselor, and the owner of All American Property Maintenance.

Made in the USA
Coppell, TX
26 February 2021